Luke shifted, inched closer, until his mouth hovered next to her cheek.

"I'm not the only guy you know. Why show up in front of me, taunting me?"

Warm puffs of air brushed against her skin. "I didn't know where else to go."

"Not good enough." The words sounded tough but there was no heat behind them.

"I knew you were more than you claimed to be." She'd always known. His unwillingness to tell her was part of what broke them apart.

"Meaning?"

"I knew if you thought I was out there you'd follow me."

Luke's head snapped back. "What makes you so sure of that?"

"Because, while I never really knew you, I did understand you. You're one of the good guys. A rescuer at heart."

HELENKAY DIMON

UNDER THE GUN

TORONTO • NEW YORK • LONDON
AMSTERDAM • PARIS • SYDNEY • HAMBURG
STOCKHOLM • ATHENS • TOKYO • MILAN • MADRID
PRAGUE • WARSAW • BUDAPEST • AUCKLAND

To Ethan Ellenberg for convincing me to give romantic suspense a serious try.

ISBN-13: 978-0-373-74517-3

UNDER THE GUN

This edition published by arrangement with Harlequin Books S.A.

For questions and comments about the quality of this book please contact us at Customer_eCare@Harlequin.ca.

www.eHarlequin.com

Printed in U.S.A.

ABOUT THE AUTHOR

Award-winning author HelenKay Dimon spent twelve years in the most unromantic career ever—divorce lawyer. After dedicating all of that effort to helping people terminate relationships, she is thrilled to deal in happy endings and write romance novels for a living. Now her days are filled with gardening, writing, reading and spending time with her family in and around San Diego. HelenKay loves hearing from readers, so stop by her Web site at www.helenkaydimon.com and say hello.

Books by HelenKay Dimon

HARLEQUIN INTRIGUE

1196—UNDER THE GUN

CAST OF CHARACTERS

Luke Hathaway—When the woman who walked out on him right before their wedding drops back into his life two years later, undercover agent Luke doesn't know whether to believe her, arrest her or act out that revenge he's planned for so long.

Claire Samson—On the run and accused of murder, Claire has limited options. She turns for help to the one man who hates her. To reach Luke she'll have to divulge the secrets that once drove them apart.

Phil Samson—Claire's ex-husband. He's wealthy, powerful and supposedly dead...but is he?

Steve Samson—Phil's brother always treated Claire well. What first seemed like grief over Phil's death has turned into something very different. He's acting odd and secretive. Suddenly he seems more dangerous than supportive.

Holden Price—Luke's best friend and a fellow agent. Holden does not trust many people, and Claire is no exception.

Adam Wright—A computer genius and Luke's partner, Adam is determined to find out the truth about Claire and save Luke from joining Claire's ex-husband in the morgue.

Chapter One

Luke Hathaway scanned the surveillance monitors set up in the nondescript Washington, D.C., office building's underground security headquarters. The wall of television screens showed every inch of public area and private offices of the financial firm on the eighteenth floor.

He and partner Adam Wright had flashed a fake subpoena ten minutes earlier. The official-looking paper convinced the guard to give up his comfortable seat and call someone in charge for guidance. That provided Adam with just enough time to slide into the chair, tap into the system and send the feed directly back to Luke's office across town.

Luke put his palm on the console and leaned in close to the monitors. The move blocked the guard's line of sight and gave Luke a good look at every angle of the business on the small screens. "Seems only the bathrooms are sacred in that place. Every other square foot has a camera hidden somewhere."

"Yeah, no paranoia there," Adam said.

The security guard covered the phone's mouthpiece. "What are you two doing? You can't touch the equipment."

"Just looking." Luke smiled at just how easy it was to infiltrate a company in supposed lockdown.

Adam had tried to tap into the computer's hard drive from back at the office but needed direct access to the financial company's internal system. One cover story and a stack of forged documents later, they were in. Just proved Luke's theory that when the back door refused to budge, you used the front. He found that most people with something to hide spent their time covering all the tough routes to information and missed the obvious ones like an overweight fifty-year-old security guard who nearly wet himself at the sight of a sheet of paper with a big seal on it.

"Now *there*'s something worth watching." Adam let out a low whistle and hitched his chin at the screen to Luke's right. "The lady with the fine—"

Luke saw the flash of jeans out of the corner of his eye. "Yeah, I can see."

Adam laughed. "It's your lack of enthusiasm that has me concerned."

Even in black and white Luke saw long dark hair and an impressive shape. Still, he needed Adam to focus on the job so they could get out of there before the guard hung up the phone and figured out what was going on.

"Drool on your own time." Luke returned to memorizing the area around the receptionist's desk in the financial office upstairs. But a prickling sensation at the base of his neck pulled his attention back to the image of the woman at the elevator.

There was something familiar about her. Something about her perfect posture with shoulders back and chin lifted high, almost daring anyone to question her. That curvy shape, from her full breasts to her slim waist to the way her dark jeans hugged her hips.

Something…

Just then she turned around and stared straight into the security camera. Didn't even pretend not to notice the device in the black bubble hanging above her head. Big eyes. Flirty smile. Hands resting on her hips in a way sure to highlight the rocking body underneath that slim-fitting T-shirt.

The hair was darker but Luke would know her face anywhere. Hard not to recognize the woman who dumped him right before their wedding two years ago. The same woman now on the run and wanted for murder.

"Is that…?" Adam came up out of the chair and pressed his face close to the screen.

The woman always did have the worst timing. "Yeah."

"Man, it can't be."

Luke fought off the urge to throw something. "Definitely is."

The security guard dropped the phone and joined Adam at the desk. "Who is she?"

Adam shook his head as if unable to believe his eyes. "Claire Samson."

Luke mentally skipped ahead to his next move. Analyzing how and why Claire had dropped right in front of him could wait. Catching her was the priority here.

He reached into his jacket pocket, grateful he'd worn a suit and brought the microphone just in case. "Got it."

"What are you doing?" Adam asked.

"Washing my car. What do you think?" Luke slipped the tiny disk in his ear and tapped it to test its strength. "We're good to go."

"Care to fill me in on where?" Adam asked.

Luke pointed at the screen. "You are staying here and watching her. I'm going to get out there and grab her before she runs again."

The guard looked back and forth between them. "Isn't she an escaped convict or something?"

"The official term is 'person of interest,'" Adam said.

Enough talk. "Adam, your job is to tell me exactly where she goes. If she moves, I want to know it. You're my eyes on this."

The guard shook his head. "Her photo's been all over the news for the past two weeks. We need to call someone or…wait. Are you the guys we call?"

Luke knew better than to sit around and debate the issue. The one thing he was an expert on was watching Claire leave. Give her a couple of minutes head start and she would slip into a crowd and disappear.

Adam grabbed Luke's arm before he could take off. "She clearly knows you're on-site. She wants your attention."

Oh, she has it. "Looks that way, yeah."

Even now while working this other job, watching an idiot businessman who made his chief financial officer disappear, Luke had been thinking about Claire and where she might be. About how he could drag her back to Virginia and put her in jail.

"It isn't our job to go after Claire. We're on this..." Adam shot the guard a scowl before lowering his voice. "We have another assignment, Luke. We need to stay here and let the police handle Claire."

Luke had tried that. He had sat back and watched law enforcement lose her trail. No way was he letting her walk out on him again. There was only one reason for her to be in this building, a place she didn't belong, on this day. She was following him. She wanted him to notice and come after her. He was happy to oblige.

When she hit the elevator button Luke knew his time was up. "I'm going after her. Do not call anyone official about her, hear me? She's mine."

He waited until Adam nodded before pushing open the door and hitting the emergency stairs at a run. Claire chose some millionaire over him—fine. Killing the guy, taking his money and trying to disappear—not fine.

"She's on the elevator," Adam said.

Luke adjusted the small speaker in his ear. "Bring up the schematics and tell me how many exits there are to this building."

"You don't know she's leaving. She could duck into an office on another floor and wait you out."

"Wrong." Luke made the prediction as he took the stairs two steps at a time. "She's headed for the street. Her plan is to blend into the lunch crowd and metro commuters roaming around McPherson Square."

Then she'd be gone. The woman was playing some kind of game. Luke knew that much. Why else was she hanging around the

D.C. metro area, instead of taking the money and heading for a country that wouldn't extradite her back for trial?

No, Claire had some sort of plot in mind. Something that involved him. Boy, would she be disappointed, because once he had her he was done running around after Claire Samson for any reason other than to turn her in to the police.

"She stepped off on the second floor and is headed toward the stairwell on the east side," Adam said.

"Exactly what I would do." It was the smart thing to do, and Claire was not dumb. As she came down the stairs, he went up. After one flight Luke stopped and stood at the door to the garage level. "Where next?"

"She's out on the first floor walking toward the west-side stairwell now. Looks like she's zigzagging."

Luke took the stairs to the lobby floor two at a time. "Can she get outside?"

Computer keys clicked before Adam answered. "Once she hits the lobby, she can turn to her right and take a service exit that dumps her in an alley off K Street."

Luke pressed the disk tighter against his ear. "Gates, locks, people? Anything there to stop her?"

"Once she's outside her only choice is a long alley to the sidewalk. She won't be able to turn around and reenter the building without a code."

Busy downtown street and one with loads of business traffic at this time of day. *Definitely not dumb.* "Got it."

"She's in the lobby now," Adam said.

Luke shoved open the door to the opposite end of the large area. The force sent it banging against the wall. Heads turned. Two people standing nearby stopped talking. Luke ignored all but the brunette at the other end of the lobby. She didn't even glance around, proving she had her escape route planned.

"Claire!" His voice bounced off the stone walls.

When their eyes met, Claire went still.

He pointed at her. "Do not move."

A hush fell over the businesspeople

gathered at the elevators. Everyone glanced around and shuffled their feet as if embarrassed by being caught in the middle of a private conversation. Despite that, they listened in, but no one seemed to notice a notorious fugitive standing right there in front of them.

"Help! He's following me." The words barely left Claire's mouth and she was off. She threw open the door to the exit and let it slam shut behind her.

The race was on.

Luke ran past a security guard, ignoring the shouts to stop. Using a shoulder, Luke knocked a twenty-something male Good Samaritan to the floor when he tried to block the path to Claire. People crowded around Luke to slow him down. He dodged, even jumped over a chair someone threw in his way.

A high-pitched alarm blared through the building as he hit the door Claire had used for her escape. The piercing sound echoed throughout the lobby, making it impossible for Luke to hear Adam screaming directions in his ear.

But Luke didn't need any help from here. Even through the harsh scent of the alley, he could smell her familiar flowery shampoo. He was right behind Claire. As long as he grabbed her before she got to the street he was good.

He looked around for anything to stick in the door and slow down any do-gooders who decided to follow him out there. The piece of wood under his foot wasn't perfect, but it might buy him some time. He shoved it through the door handle, then raced down the pavement, following Claire and getting closer with each step.

She kept her body toned, probably from hours of aerobics like before, but he was still faster. Only a few feet away now, he could see her on the other side of the Dumpster, hear her heavy breathing and watch her hair fly around in the warm October breeze. Then she slid to a stop. Actually lost her footing and fell back on one hand.

Instead of getting up and breaking out of the dark alley into the sunshine and possible freedom, she scrambled to her feet and ran toward him with her cheeks puffing and eyes wild. She landed with a thump against his chest but didn't stop moving. With her hands wrapped in his shirt, she tugged him toward the door and back into the building they'd just left.

"We have to move," she said. "Inside. Now."

Luke planted his feet to stop the slide across the loose gravel under him. "Claire, stop."

She grabbed his jacket sleeve and pulled hard enough to rip the fabric at the shoulder. "No time. We have to get out of here."

Luke looked at the shadowed figure standing near the distant sidewalk. From the bulk, Luke knew it was a man, but that was all. "Who the hell is that?"

"I don't know," she said, her usually husky voice interrupted by huge gulping breaths.

Luke knew there was no way back into the building without a code, and he sure didn't have it. They had to go through the guy at the other end.

"Tell security to back off!" Luke yelled the order loud enough for Adam to pick up through the honking horns and other sounds of the nearby street.

"Who are you talking to?" Claire asked.

The shadow at the end of the alley moved closer. The figure took his hand out of his windbreaker pocket. The sun behind him glinted off the metal of his gun. The baseball cap pulled over his face hid his identity, but the casual clothes and quiet stalking told Luke they had a problem. This other guy was no cop.

Luke positioned his body in front of Claire's. A bullet or knife or anything else would have to go through him first.

He could hear people on the other side of the building's door and a dull thud as they pushed against it. He needed backup and a way out that didn't involve fighting through an angry crowd that viewed him as Claire's attacker.

"He with you?" Luke asked her over his shoulder.

"Does he look happy to see me?"

Adam's voice crackled in Luke's ear. "Luke, there aren't any security guards outside. They're all standing around the lobby with their thumbs up—"

"Then who's this guy I'm looking at?" Luke heard a short buzzing and saw the outside camera switch position to aim at the end of the alley.

The other man pulled his cap even lower. The gun pointed down, but Luke knew that could change in a second and didn't wait. He shoved Claire behind the Dumpster, ignoring her squeal of surprise. The mystery guy's footsteps fell faster against the pavement now. Luke ducked and squeezed in next to Claire.

Her eyes grew wide when he slipped out the gun he had tucked at the small of his back. "Where did you get that?" she asked.

"Not important."

"You told me you sold art for a living."

"I find antiques." That was his cover and he was sticking to it.

"Find them or shoot them?"

Luke ignored the sarcasm and checked his gun. "This is your last chance to tell me the truth. Do you know how to do that?"

"You may want to remember I'm wanted for murder. Ticking me off might not be your best move."

As if he could forget that fact. "Who's this guy coming after you?"

"Don't know." Her skin paled. "Probably someone Phil sent."

Phil Samson. Her husband. Make that her *dead* husband. Luke vowed to deal with her lies later. Now he needed to get them out of there alive.

The other man's steps stopped. Except for the soft rustle of his slick jacket, he didn't make a sound. But Luke could feel the tension radiating off the guy. He motioned for Claire to stay quiet as he peeled her fingers off his shirt. The last thing he needed was her slowing him down.

Glaring at her one last time, Luke mentally started the countdown. In one swift move he stood up and pivoted around the Dumpster, gun raised, to face the other man head on. The guy's eyes bugged out the second before he lifted his weapon. The slight hesitation gave Luke the opening he needed. His bullet hit the man's shoulder, sending him stumbling backward.

At the sharp bang people gathered at the end of the alley. Someone shouted for the police. Another person started yelling about a robbery. Luke heard it all, but his focus remained locked on the man in front of him. The guy refused to go down easy. Instead, he held on to his weapon and stayed on his feet.

Claire ran for the back door to the building and yanked on it. It took her a few tugs to see the wood Luke had shoved there. With a growl of frustration she ripped it out.

When the door still refused to open, she hammered it with her fists. "Open up!"

Luke lunged for her. "Claire, no! It's—"

The other man's roar cut off the rest of Luke's warning. Everything moved in a blur. Claire jumped away from the door, holding the stick in her hand like a bat. At the same time the mystery man lurched, shifting his gun to waist height.

When the man pivoted toward Claire, Luke didn't hesitate. No way was he going to let the guy get a shot off in her direction. Luke shoved her against the wall as he fired a second shot at the attacker. The explosion from the gun mixed with a second crack Luke couldn't place. For a moment all he heard was the whir of distant sirens and screams from the street.

As he watched the man drop to his knees,

the twitching began. Luke tried to flex his hand to keep it from going to sleep, but the muscles fell limp. Heat raged in a line down to his fingers as if every nerve ending had caught fire under his skin.

Claire picked that moment to run out of her hiding place with the stick held high. She slammed it into the back of the other man's neck, knocking him face-first into the gravel.

"Claire, what are you—"

Grunting with a mania Luke guessed was fueled by adrenaline, she finally faced him. Her gaze zoomed in on his arm and her cheeks blanched even more.

"Are you okay?" Her question came out in a voice both breathy and uneven.

He had no idea what she was asking or why. "Fine."

"You've been shot."

"I…what?" Luke caught her around the waist to keep her from running. His head spun and his vision blurred, but he knew he had to hold on. No way was he losing her this time. Only thing was, she didn't struggle or try to break away. He couldn't figure out that part.

"Luke, stop moving around."

"You recognize that guy now?" Luke asked, forcing the words out over the sudden searing pain radiating through his shoulder.

She stared at the man lying at her feet with the bullet hole in his back. When she glanced back at Luke's face, her hand tightened on his forearm. "You have to sit down."

"Why?" With the noise at the end of the alley and police sirens blaring, Luke knew they had to move. "Doesn't matter. It's time to get out of here."

As the whirring screech from the approaching police cars grew louder, two men started down the alley. Luke guessed the body sprawled on the ground grabbed their attention. He couldn't blame them for wanting to check it out. Still, he had his fill of knuckleheads rushing in and trying to save Claire.

"Stay back." Luke tried to lift his hurt arm, but a new bolt of pain blinded him, forcing him to let it fall uselessly to his side. He finally looked down and saw the blood. "What the hell?"

"You can't feel that?"

The thumping increased. “I can now.”

“You’re injured.” She ripped the bottom edge of her T-shirt and held it against his shoulder. “Badly.”

The pressure of her palm knocked the breath out of him. He bit back the shout rumbling around in his throat and forced out the words he needed to say. “Adam, get here now.”

Claire glanced around. “Who are you talking to?”

A white van appeared at the end of the alley a few seconds later. Adam got out, flashed his fake badge and started issuing orders.

“Our ride is here,” Luke said through teeth tight with agony.

“Where are we going?” Claire shifted her attention from the commotion back to him.

“Out of here.”

“Not to the police.”

“Not yet.” He vowed to get the real answers first.

It was about time Claire Samson learned there were consequences to her actions. He was the perfect person to teach her—as long as he didn’t pass out first.

Chapter Two

A half hour later Claire heard Luke hiss as he shrugged out of his suit jacket and got the material caught on his watch. He sat on his kitchen table with his legs dangling and his dress shirt unbuttoned down to his stomach. The only blemish on his bare skin came from the dark red stain spreading across the white material.

Slumped shoulders and face drawn tight with pain, Luke looked ready to drop. Claire half hoped he would. If he fell over she could run. Well, she could if she somehow managed to knock out Luke's friend. Mr. Blond, Big and Ticked Off. Yeah, that guy looked ready to kill someone, namely her.

Both men had chests and shoulders broad enough to make football players jealous.

Luke's light brown hair with bangs that brushed his eyebrows gave a boyish quality to his handsomeness. But in the two years since they were together he had changed. He now possessed a lethal air, making him more like his tough friend than the charming man she once thought would be her future.

Neither man gave off the upper-crust snootiness she expected from guys who supposedly spent their days locating precious works of art. She doubted Luke could tell a Chagall from a cartoon. The comfortable gunplay made her think his work was something more along the lines of law enforcement, but he lacked the clean-cut government-man look she associated with FBI agents. Now that she had experienced the great misfortune of being questioned by a few, she recognized the beast.

One thing was for sure. Luke, the man she followed from a distance and tracked to the office building—the same one who ran her down in the alley and kept a gun in his waistband—did not spend much time behind a desk. She'd bet her life on that. In fact, that's exactly what she was doing.

She needed Luke's help and cooperation,

wanted to get him interested in her case and set him loose to find the truth. She just had the tiny problem of earning his trust first. With their history that was going to take some time, and probably some begging, which was not her strongest skill.

Luke focused on his friend. “You can get me the whiskey. The rest of the supplies are in the bathroom.”

“You’re thirsty?” she asked. “Now?”

Luke ignored her and kept talking to his friend or partner or whatever the other man was. “Then you’ve got to get back to the scene and help clean up the mess with the police.”

The guy shot Claire a blank stare. “I’m not leaving you alone with her.”

“My name is Claire.”

The man made a face as if he’d tasted something sour. “I know who you are.”

“Adam, meet Claire, and vice versa.” Luke peeled off his shirt, gasping when the blood-soaked material caught on his skin. “The supplies? And now would be good.”

Adam nodded, then headed down the hall.

The second they were alone Luke pinned

her with the same green-eyed gaze that used to make her forget what she was saying.

"If you even try to move out of this room, I'll stop you," he said.

"You only have one good arm."

"I can do a lot with that."

Which was exactly why she hadn't yet made a run for the door. "I'm not leaving."

"That's not my experience," he muttered under his breath.

Adam stalked back into the room and dumped a small box on the table, along with gauze, some medicine, a knife and a bottle. "What are we looking at in terms of injuries here?"

Luke tried to lift his arm but groaned, instead. "It's a through and through. Not serious. Just bloody and stings like a son of a bitch."

She eyed the whiskey. "Which is cause for a celebratory drink?"

Both men stared at her but only Luke answered. "I'm going to use it to clean the wound."

She noticed his husky voice had cleared and his swaying had stopped. Still…

"Shouldn't you be at a hospital? I mean, how bad is this?"

Luke picked up a bandage packet and put the edge between his teeth and ripped it open. "It's a gunshot, so it doesn't feel good. But unfortunately for you, I'm not going to die."

She forgot how dizzying his stubbornness could be. "You are if you don't stop with the attitude."

He peeked up at her through his mop of hair. "I'd like to remind you how I got shot."

That was an easy one. He refused to stick with the mental plan she had worked out for him. He might hate her, but his rescue tendencies hadn't dulled.

"Have we figured out who it was you two killed?" Adam asked.

Luke nodded in her direction. "Ask her."

They both stared at her, but she ignored it. Her mind wandered back to that alley. The acrid mix of blood and sweat filled her nose. For a second there Claire had forgotten this death was on her. She actually had killed a man this time. It was in self-defense and in an effort to save Luke, but someone was still dead.

She swallowed hard to keep from gagging on the bile that rushed up the back of her throat. "He was following me. I don't know who he was."

"Your partner?" Luke crumpled the empty packet in his fist. "I'm betting you weren't really the victim out there today."

If she thought for one minute Luke intended to save her when she walked into that alley…yeah, not the case. He hunted her down for one reason only—to turn her over to the police. She could see it in the intensity of his eyes.

He had been in that building for a job of some sort. Hung out on every floor until the security cameras finally flared to life. She showed up hoping to get his attention, but she'd miscalculated. She expected he would catch a glimpse and get the bug to start digging into her story. She hadn't been prepared for a multifloor rundown that ended with a shoot-out.

The entire situation made her want to scream. Phil did this. He set her up, pretended to be dead and now had someone on her tail. Marrying him had been the worst decision of her life.

Adam spilled the alcohol on Luke's wound, earning an impressive string of yelled profanity in return.

Men. "You're going to kill him. Here, let me." She pushed Adam out of the way. Kind of felt good to surprise the guy with a shove.

Then she stepped between Luke's open legs, resting her thigh against his. The reality of being separated by only two thin pieces of material made her freeze in place. An accidental brush against him shouldn't mean anything. Certainly shouldn't send her stomach into flip-flop mode.

"What are you doing?" Luke asked.

"Helping." She sucked in a few deep breaths as she struggled for control. Even after all this time he had the power to shatter her into a thousand useless pieces.

Instead of dwelling on her weakness to a man so determined to forget her, she went to work. Grabbing the gauze out of his hand, she rubbed the swab over the jagged wound with infinite care. When his lips stayed pinched, she knew the whirling in her stomach only went one way.

Adam plunked down in the chair beside

her. His gaze never left her hands. It was as if he expected her to injure Luke with a cotton ball.

"You have a problem with me?" she asked.

Adam's eyebrow lifted. "Other than the fact you killed your husband?"

Nothing like being found guilty without a trial. "Allegedly killed."

"Does it sound better to you when you make that distinction?"

"Answer this, Adam. Do you always judge people you don't know?"

Luke exhaled. "Maybe you two could spar another time. Like when I'm not bleeding to death."

"I see you've taken up exaggeration." She worked on Luke's arm, ignoring the pain that flashed in his eyes as she swiped the pad over his injury with delicate care. "Not a very attractive quality, by the way."

"Yeah, well, it's a hobby." Luke leaned over and tried to grab for something from the table. The move put his head right by her cheek and close enough for his breath to tickle her ear.

As soon as his hair brushed her skin, he sat up straight. Even grunted.

The quick move broke her trance. “What now?”

“Hand me the needle and tape.” He barked out the order.

And she ignored it.

He sent her a wide-eyed surprised look. “I’m bleeding here.”

“I’ll get it.” This time Adam did the shoving. Without any fanfare he crowded Claire to the side and away from Luke. Before Luke could argue, Adam started sewing. “You need anything else right now?”

“An explanation from Claire here would be good,” Luke said.

She glanced at the syringe and bottles sitting on the table. “I was just thinking the same thing.”

Luke’s skin whitened as Adam worked. With each tug of the thread and poke through his skin, Luke’s mouth stretched flatter into a thin line. His jaw tightened to the point of breaking.

“I’ll take her to the police after this.” Adam ignored Luke’s squirming. “We should end this now and get back to work.”

She decided to focus on the latter point.

"And exactly what is your work? You were clearly looking for something in that building and it wasn't me. Wasn't a painting, either."

"Speaking of that." Adam put a hand on his hip and stared her down. "How did you know we'd be at that building?"

She'd stalked Luke, of course, but admitting that was out of the question. "I got lucky."

Adam snorted. "Right."

"Don't worry about Claire and her snooping. I've got this situation under control," Luke said.

Situation? She assumed that was his new pet name for her. Interesting how he couldn't use his arm and was six seconds away from passing out but still thought he was in charge. Only the Y chromosome could result in that kind of bent logic.

Luke inhaled. "Just call the office—"

"You mean your antique storefront or your real job…" She hesitated until she knew she had their joint attention. "Whatever that job actually is."

Luke scowled in her direction before turning back to Adam. "Go back to the scene," he said. "Claire and I are going to have a little talk."

She noticed Luke sounded more like police and less antique expert by the minute. "I'm fine, but thanks."

"Then?" Adam asked.

"I'll bring her in."

"Never going to happen." And she meant it. Injury or not, she would knock Luke down, press against his wound. Do whatever it took to stay free.

The idea of sitting in a cell and depending on the services of a court-appointed defense attorney made her head spin with fear. She knew how the system worked—poor people lost. Despite everything she had done in the last two years to escape her past, she had somehow slipped back into a situation where she had nothing. The exact place she'd spent her entire adult life trying to avoid.

"One more thing." Luke used his good hand to cuff Adam's shoulder. "This all stays between us."

"How exactly do I explain the dead guy in the alley?"

Claire shook her head. Antiques experts. *Right.*

"You'll think of something. I just need a little time with Claire."

"How much?"

"Some. Might need a cover, too." When Adam started to argue, Luke stopped him. "This isn't up for debate."

Silence lingered while Adam just stood there. When he finally spoke again, he sounded anything but convinced. "You've got twenty-four hours."

Luke nodded. "Agreed."

"Not by me," she muttered.

"Just be careful." Adam grabbed his keys but not before shooting Claire one last warning glare.

She waited until the door closed to say anything. "I get the distinct impression your friend doesn't like me."

"And here I thought you weren't good at reading people."

She picked up a damp towel and wiped the area around Luke's wound before taping a bandage over Adam's surprisingly professional stitching. The process took a few minutes. Rather than haggle and argue, she used the quiet to come up with a plan to leave Luke before Adam's twenty-four-hour deadline expired.

She saw the mess of ripped paper and blood-drenched pads on the table. "You've ignored this question so far, but care to tell me why a businessman keeps a syringe in his bathroom?"

He smiled in a way that was more warning than welcoming. "Why? Want to learn a new way to get rid of your next husband?"

"I see you've decided to be as much of a jerk as possible." She threw the towel on the table and plunked down in the chair Adam had abandoned.

"Some people like me," Luke said.

She didn't doubt that one bit. From creeping around and watching him for the past few weeks, she knew about his dating life. Women came over, stayed the night, and a new one showed up a few nights later. It was an endless parade of blondes and brunettes, each one looking easier than the one before her.

But that wasn't Claire's business. Her focus

was on clearing her name. Like it or not, she needed help for that. When the whole town judged you guilty, you had to find someone who didn't. Luke didn't fit in that believer category yet, but she hoped he would.

"What's the plan now?" she asked.

"You tell me what happened to your husband."

She hated that word because it made Phil sound special, and he wasn't. "And then?"

"I'll decide that after I hear what you have to say."

"How is that fair?"

"Do you have a choice?"

She didn't.

Chapter Three

Four hours and two confusing explanations from Claire later, Luke was ready for a handful of painkillers and a bed. But thanks to his unwanted female sidekick, he didn't have the option of the sweet oblivion of sleep.

They stood at the double doors to his office suite. He positioned his body in front of Claire to block her as much as possible from the security cameras he knew were shooting them from all angles.

Following her gaze, he looked at the words stamped on the door: Recovery Project. On the outside, the fifth-floor office on a side street in the Georgetown area of Washington, D.C., housed an antiques salvage operation. In reality it served as headquarters for an off-the-books agency tasked with finding missing people, both those who wanted to hide and those who prayed for rescue. That's what he did for a living. He hunted people.

Since he didn't directly work for the government, he didn't have to obey its stringent rules. The Recovery Project was the place the guys with the real badges came when they needed the dirty work done. Luke and his team worked outside the law. They flashed fake credentials or whatever else it took to get in the door and never asked for credit when they succeeded in reaching their goals. To Luke's way of thinking, they accomplished more in one day than most law-enforcement agencies could manage during a year-long sting operation.

Lights on the security panel flickered when he swiped his key card through the reader. The doors to the main reception area opened with a click. The place was in after-hours mode, dark except for one small lamp in the lobby area. Just as he expected—quiet and empty. It was about time something worked right today.

He had called seven times on the way over,

trying the main number and then each private line to make sure they'd be alone. The idea was to protect Claire's secret for a few more hours. The gun tucked into his sling protected him from her. If she made a move in any direction he didn't like, he was ready.

Not that he could shoot her. Despite everything that happened between them before and everything bubbling under the surface now, physically hurting her was out of the question. But the desire for emotional revenge had not dulled since she'd left him holding a stack of bills for a wedding that never happened.

He had spent those first days dreaming of her coming back to him broken and despondent, begging his forgiveness for leaving. In his fantasy, he turned her away. He would listen, laugh in her face and walk off. That proved to be much harder in real life. Those chocolate-brown eyes and body born for the bedroom were enough to drive any sane man to do something really stupid. She had done it to him. Likely did it to most men unlucky enough to cross her path.

No, he couldn't push her out of his head.

But he could threaten. Oh, boy, could he threaten.

"What is this place?" She walked up to the receptionist's desk and fingered the business cards piled there in individual holders.

He started to follow her and groaned when the swift shuffle to the side sent pain rippling down his injured arm. "My employer."

"Ready to tell me what you really do for a living?" She glanced around at the stark white walls that gleamed despite the relative darkness. "Seems sort of modern for a place that supposedly deals in antiques."

"We find them. We don't collect them."

"For some reason I doubt you do either of those things."

When she leaned against the counter, her hair caught the light. Mahogany replaced the rich brown color he remembered. He guessed the longer, darker look was part of her disguise. Little did she know, all the dye in the world couldn't cover her high cheekbones and smooth skin. Purple or green hair, he would know her anywhere.

"Let's move on to a conversation I actually care about. Your missing husband," Luke said.

"Former."

Luke refused to let that distinction matter. "The divorce is final, but the financial settlement wasn't signed. That's the point of the murder, wasn't it?" When she ducked her head, he lowered his to meet her eyes. "Right? With Phil dead and the money issues not resolved, you would inherit. With Phil alive and the agreement signed, you got whatever the prenup and final paperwork said."

"I see you've been reading the newspaper again." She picked up a business card and tapped it end over end against the counter.

"You would have been a very rich widow." He watched the card twirl faster between her fingers. "You know, if you hadn't actually been caught in the act."

"I was set up."

"Tell me again why I'm supposed to believe that."

"We've been through this. I told you the entire story twice on the way over here."

He folded his hand over hers. The goal was to stop the annoying clicking of card against counter before his head exploded. At the touch, he felt a shot of a different kind.

The feel of her soft hand beneath his brought back a flood of memories. Skin against skin, touching her, making love to her. He didn't even have to close his eyes to picture her sprawled naked across his white sheets.

When the image refused to leave his mind, he shook his head to knock it out. He also pulled back his hand, because touching her skin was just plain stupid.

"Let's go to my office," he said.

"This should be interesting."

That was just about the last word he'd use. But rather than debate, he slid his fingers under her elbow and steered her down the short hallway to his room. Letting her peek into an area so private made him nervous, but it was better to bring her here than drag her to his house. Here he would stay focused and he could make sure she only saw what he wanted her to see.

The conference rooms, computer rooms and most of the back half of the space were off-limits to visitors and anyone else who failed to get through the retinal scanner and other security measures in place there. That included Claire. Especially Claire.

He swiped his key card at the second door on the left and punched in his code. When the door unlocked, he gestured for her to move inside ahead of him.

The spare and minimalist look of the rest of the space continued in here. No dark heavy wood or oil paintings featuring somber sixteenth-century faces. He preferred clean lines, a comfortable leather chair and a desk sturdy enough to hold the stacks of documents piled on top of it.

Not that the papers contained anything of value. Everything on his desk was there for show. The actual work files sat secured in his hidden safe along with his removable computer hard drive and every other piece of confidential information from his cases. She would see what he wanted her to see and nothing else.

He waved at the black chair in front of his desk and took his seat behind it. With his computer switched on and his mind engaged, he was ready to hear her story one more time.

"Again," he said.

"You're going to type with one hand?"

Her reminder made his arm ache even more.

Thanks to her presence, he had to skip the heavy-duty painkillers and go with antibiotics and aspirin for the injury. The combination wasn't working. Every nerve ending throbbed.

"I'll get by." He stared across the desk right into her dark eyes. In that moment he wondered if he really would survive a second round with her. Last time she won, but he vowed to be the victor this time.

IF HE WANTED to be some sort of martyr and plow ahead with questions when he should be in a hospital, Claire wasn't about to argue. She needed his help. If she tried to tell him how to provide it, his testosterone would kick in and she'd never get through this uneasy alliance.

"It was three weeks ago. Phil called and asked me to come to the house," she explained.

"Is that normal?"

"I don't understand the question."

Luke leaned back in his chair. Held on to his injured arm while he did it. "According to everything I've read, the divorce wasn't exactly amicable."

She had known the accusations would come eventually. Still, the idea that Luke so readily believed the absolute worst of her stung. "You mean because Phil told everyone who would listen that I was a whore."

"I was trying to be tactful."

"Why start now?"

"Fine." Luke tapped his fingers against the space bar on his keyboard. "He accused you of sleeping around."

"I didn't."

Luke hesitated before tapping again. "Okay."

"You believe me?" Something deep inside her chest tightened into a hard ball while waiting for the answer. It was as if every cell waited to see what he would say.

Instead, he waved his hand in a dismissive gesture. "It's not important. Not my business."

Yeah, well, it mattered to her. But she refused to justify or explain. If Luke was so determined to judge her guilty on that point, let him. She knew she had damaged his ego when she walked out. A man didn't forgive that sort of thing easily. But no matter how much he hated her, the important thing was that he believe in her story enough to help her.

"Why did you go to the house?" he asked.

"It was stupid." In hindsight, the dumbest move of her life, even less intelligent than her marriage. "Phil called and said he wanted to come to a reasonable financial resolution. Asked me to come over to talk. I should have questioned the change in him, but I was so relieved. And when I got there everything was wrong."

The scene unfolded in her mind. The dark first floor. Music playing in the background. The strong odor of cleaner. She had called Phil's name from the front door, but no one answered. When she heard a thump upstairs she figured he was moving stuff around and couldn't hear her. She followed the curving stairway to the second floor. There was a light on the landing and more spilling out of the master bedroom down the hall.

"I walked into our old bedroom. Something seemed off. My jewelry was on the bed, the same items Phil insisted I stole when I left the first time. He must have had them all along."

"Anything else? Was anyone there?"

The remembered smell filled her head. It was a mix of sickening sweetness and harsh cleanser. The same wave of dizziness that hit her that night flowed through her again.

She could hear the floor creak as Luke shifted around in his seat. She knew she was safe in his office, but she couldn't pull her mind from the memory.

"Just relax and tell me what you saw."

Luke moved his hand over hers. She didn't even realize she had twisted a business card in her palm until Luke slipped it out from between her fingers and put it on the desk.

As soon as the warmth of his skin came, it left again. His hand was back at his keyboard, but the touch had returned her to the present. She could finish the story. She *had* to finish.

"There was blood splattered on the walls and on the floor. I remember kneeling, looking around trying to figure out what I was seeing. Then I heard the sirens."

"The police."

"Yeah, but it still didn't sink in. Even seeing the cleaning bucket didn't compute."

"And that's where the police found you."

"On the floor by the bloodstain."

"They say you killed Phil and hid the body." Luke's hand hovered over the keys. "That they caught you cleaning up the scene."

"But they conveniently forget that Phil made a call from the house only a short time before that." She scoffed. "I mean, did he turn into smoke or something?"

Luke nodded. "Admittedly, the timeline is going to be the prosecution's weakness at trial."

"Gee, thanks for the vote of confidence. Maybe you should be on my defense team."

"Tell me what happened."

"Phil set me up with a brilliance I didn't know he had in him. He called his brother that night and claimed I broke in." The prosecutor depended on the delay in calls from Phil to Steve to the police to explain the problem. "The theory is that I killed a 190-pound man and hid the body within a fifteen-minute window."

The evidence didn't fit. The fact that everyone refused to see that made her seethe in frustration.

"I'm assuming you deny killing him." Luke said it more as a fact than a question.

"I can't kill someone who's not dead."

Luke began typing. Even with one hand, he moved fast. Images flipped by on his screen. She could see him trying to log in passwords as fast as possible. Probably feared she would somehow break into his system.

A Web site she recognized popped up. "Wait, you're with the FBI?"

He smiled. "Definitely not."

"But you just entered a password to get on their system."

"True."

Lines of information filled his screen. She leaned in closer to see.

He eyed her for a second. "Sit back."

"But that said something about Homeland Security."

"Yeah, I know."

"We're talking about my life here, Luke."

"This is confidential information." He said

the words but didn't do anything to hide the monitor from her view.

"Then why do you have it, Mr. Antiques Expert?"

Another window opened. This one had the D.C. Police logo on it. A few more strokes and Luke entered another password. The page that popped up looked like a bank statement.

"Other than violating about a thousand state and federal laws, what are you doing?" she asked.

"Checking for evidence that Phil is alive. Phone and bank records. Something that would support your theory about Phil setting this up to make it look like you killed him so he had cover to run."

"That's exactly what happened."

Luke's gaze did not leave the monitor. "So you keep saying."

"You don't work for the FBI."

"I already said no."

"Or the police."

"Still no."

Wariness spiraled through her. He had access to all sorts of information he shouldn't have access to. "Exactly what side do you work for?"

Luke stopped typing long enough to stare at her. "Do you really care?"

"Yes." She said the word but didn't mean it. Her question wasn't about following the rules. It was about trying to figure out who he was—the man he claimed to be or the one who carried a gun.

Luke hit a few more keys and then sat back in his chair. "There's nothing on Phil. No sign of life at all. He hasn't accessed any account or anything else in the three weeks since he disappeared."

"The man is a multimillionaire."

"I seem to remember you mentioning that when you left me for him."

She dug her fingernails into the arms of the chair to keep from shaking him. "Phil has money hidden all over the place.

"None of it's moving."

Luke didn't believe her. The fact hit her with enough force to push the breath out of her lungs on a *whoosh*. Desperation bubbled in her stomach. She had to move before it ran up her throat and she embarrassed herself.

She got up and paced the few feet between her chair and the open door to the office. A few steps and she could hit the hallway, run as fast as possible for the door and hope his injury slowed him down enough to let her get away.

"Don't even think about it." Luke issued the threat without moving an inch.

If he worried that she was about to make a break for it, he sure wasn't showing it. Open hand, relaxed shoulders, even a small smile playing on this mouth. Yeah, he was sure he had her under control. She saw it in every line of his body.

He was hiding more than his real profession. Behind the passwords and key cards there might not be an easy way out of what looked like an otherwise normal office. Still, she had to try.

She moved her foot closer to the hallway to test her theory. If the door slammed shut and locked her in, she'd deal with his anger then. It wasn't as if Luke trusted her, anyway. He probably expected her to bolt. Was waiting for it.

She inched the same foot outside the

office. Her gaze stayed locked on Luke. He taunted her by leaning back further into his oversize leather chair. With one last deep breath she stepped out of the doorway. She turned her head to look down the hall.

A second later the barrel of a gun pressed hard against her forehead. She bit back a scream as she stared into the blue eyes of a stranger dressed all in black.

Adrenaline pumping, she raised her hands in surrender. "It's okay. I'm here with Luke."

The other man's smile never reached his eyes. "Luke who?"

Chapter Four

Blood thundered in Claire's ears. If her heart drummed any harder, it would come right out of her chest and land on the floor at her feet.

With Luke injured and her without a weapon, she tried to use reason to keep the big guy with the gun from firing straight into her forehead. "Listen to me. We can work this out."

"I doubt it." Black-haired and well over six feet, the guy radiated danger. His arm stayed straight and the gun never wavered. If ever there was a man ready to shoot first and talk later, it was him.

"You don't want to do this," she said, trying to stall for time as she mentally searched for a way out of this.

"I wouldn't be so sure about that."

At this range, there was no way the guy

would miss unless he was cross-eyed, and she was just not that lucky. Not lately. If something didn't change, she'd die with the presumption of guilt tied around her neck.

And Luke, injured and vulnerable. She didn't want to think what would happen to him. Her only hope was for the meds to wear off and his brain to kick-start him into action. That even now he had his gun drawn and was working on a plan to free them.

"Phil's just using you." She didn't have any money, her ex saw to that, but maybe this guy didn't know the intricacies of her financial settlement. Only possible if he never watched the news or read a paper.

"Phil who?"

"I can beat his price. Whatever he's giving you to do this, I'll double it." A total lie, but she was desperate to keep the conversation going and the gun's trigger exactly where it was right now.

The guy pursed his lips as if considering the deal. "Interesting."

"Problem out there?" Luke asked from inside the room.

Her heart dropped at the sound of his deep

voice. She closed her eyes in defeat. Maybe Luke really was an antiques dealer. Seemed a guy with a badge would be smart enough to understand the benefit of sneaking up on a situation like this rather than announcing his presence.

"Are you going to answer him?" the guy asked.

She thought she heard a touch of amusement in his voice, which made about as much sense as everything else that had happened in the past hour. "No."

"You should."

She took that as an order. "We have company." She shouted that obvious assessment to Luke. She wanted to tell him to bring his gun, but she was pretty sure that would tick off the guy who wanted to put a bullet through her brain.

After a bit of paper shuffling and chair squeaking, Luke appeared in the doorway. He stared down at the gun. Up at the guy. Didn't show an ounce of surprise.

"Ahhh, I see you weren't kidding."

Her hands balled into fists. "That's all you have to say?"

"No." Luke stepped into the hall and leaned against the wall. If the other man's presence worried him, he sure didn't show it. "I saw you two on the monitor."

"What monitor?" she asked.

Luke hitched his chin in the general vicinity of the gun. "Ease up. You're scaring her."

Oh, he was way past that point. "Lowering the weapon would help. I can't go anywhere, anyway."

The mystery man's shoulders relaxed. "I wouldn't let you."

"Looks like we have an agreement, then." Luke rubbed his shoulder. "Holden Price, this is the infamous Claire Samson."

"Wait, you know him?" Her heart flip-flopped at the thought. When she tried to turn her head to let Luke see just how angry she was, the gun scratched her skin. "Uh, could you call your friend off?"

Holden looked her up and down. "When I'm ready."

"Lower the weapon," Luke ordered, his voice suddenly stronger and harsher. "Now."

Holden hesitated before pulling the gun back closer to his side. "What's going on?"

"So that's a yes?" She looked back and forth between the men. What she really wanted to do was knock their heads together as payback for scaring the crap out of her. "You two do know each other."

"We both work here," Luke said.

"Now that we've cleared that up, why is she here?" Holden still held his gun at the ready. A fact that kept Claire on edge.

"We had an incident."

It was as if the testosterone had rushed to Luke's brain and swamped his common sense. She fought the urge to roll her eyes. "It's a little more than that. You were shot."

Luke shrugged on his good side. "Yeah, like I said, an incident."

"I know about the alley. I've already been there to make sure Adam has everything under control." Holden nodded in the direction of the sling. "You okay?"

Since Holden actually frowned, looking as if Luke's health mattered, Claire decided to let the gun threat slide. Luke might not understand how serious his injuries were, but from the way Holden's eyebrows snapped together she assumed he got it.

"Will be," Luke said.

The color had returned to his cheeks, but the dark circles under his eyes just kept getting darker. She was convinced he'd drop over at some point. Probably right when she'd need him to show off those impressive shooting skills of his, because that was how her life worked at the moment.

"You should be at home resting," she pointed out. "It's not normal for most people to get shot. Not even for supposed art dealers."

"Antiques," Holden muttered.

"Only way I can take the night off is to turn you over to the police. That scenario interest you?" Luke actually smirked as he made the observation. The man knew when he had a conversation won. He knew and she knew.

But she wasn't ready to give up. "Not really."

"Why did you bring her to the office?" Holden asked.

When the barrel of Holden's gun finally pointed toward the floor, instead of at any part of her, she coughed out the breath she'd been holding. "I have a bigger question. What's with all the weapons?"

Luke's hand inched toward his gun as if she had reminded him. "We like to be prepared."

"In case you encounter a dangerous collectibles shop owner?"

Holden nodded. "Something like that."

Only a man bathed in darkness who grumbled more than he spoke could throw out a line like that and make it sound menacing. Without thinking, she shifted closer to Luke. Yeah, he hated her, but he'd had the chance to shoot her in the alley and passed it up. She wasn't convinced Holden would do the same.

"What are you doing here this late?" Luke asked.

"I was in the back when the phones started ringing. The way they went a desk at a time sounded suspicious to me. Thought I'd stick around to see if we had trouble." Holden stared at her. "And we do."

"I don't want to be here, either, if that helps," she said.

Luke talked right over her. "Was just trying to see who, if anyone, was here. I had to use the computer and couldn't exactly leave her waiting in the car."

"Makes sense." Holden's lips quirked in what Claire assumed was his version of a smile. "How'd you manage to trip the alarm?"

Luke went still. "What?"

"You forget to swipe the card or something?"

"No. Followed protocol exactly."

With a suddenness that shocked her, Holden straightened. Both men morphed from relaxed interplay to an on-guard stance in an instant. Holden's gun was raised as Luke started pushing buttons on his big square watch.

She knew enough to be worried. Wide-shouldered macho men didn't spook that easily. "What is it?"

"Quiet," Luke said in a voice that hovered just above a whisper.

With guns out, they surrounded her. She couldn't move or run. The closeness suffocated her as they walked her backward into Luke's office. "What's happening?"

"You have someone with you?" Luke took a position on one side of the doorway.

With his good arm, he pushed her behind him. Since the idea of dying in a shoot-out didn't exactly appeal to her, she stayed put. They'd talk about his tendency to shove her around another time. Right now, it worked for her. "No."

Luke stared at her.

"No, really," she said. "No partners. Nothing."

His facial features took on a nasty sharpness. "We're going to take this guy out, so tell me the truth."

She knew she'd be blamed for what was happening now, whatever that was. "I just did."

"Possible you were followed?" Holden asked from the other side of the doorway.

Luke's concentration switched between his watch and the hallway. "I don't see how."

"Maybe you're off your game." Holden stood on the other side of the open door. "The injury, meeting up with your old—"

"No."

Together they made up a wall of angry brooding male. Claire couldn't hear or see anything. Except for their breathy whispers, a deadly quiet filled the office. But she knew from the way Holden and Luke held their bodies so still that something or someone very bad lingered out there waiting for them.

The reality hit her. *Phil.* Again. He had access to endless resources and a deep hatred for her. Throwing the blame on her for his mess was one thing. Having someone track her every move was another. Years before, she had seen Phil as a safe alternative to Luke. Everything about Luke was shrouded in mystery. Phil had nothing to hide. She never dreamed he would turn into her biggest nightmare.

Luke motioned for her to stand with her back against the wall behind him. "You do everything we say when we say. Got it?"

She nodded, afraid to utter even a syllable and risk having her voice carry back to whoever was out there.

Holden stared at his watch. It matched Luke's perfectly. "He's in conference room two."

She grabbed the back of Luke's shirt and tugged to get his attention. "He who?"

"Whoever is trying to kill you."

"You believe me?"

"I believe someone wants you dead. The 'why' is a question for another time."

She rested her forehead against his back for the briefest of moments. "If we live."

Luke pressed a button on the side of his watch. From over his shoulder she could see the face. Instead of the time, a floor plan flashed in green lighting. She saw four red dots in the outlined rooms. Only one of them moved.

She pitched her voice as low as possible, which was hard given the way her head buzzed with fear. "Is that him?"

"Last chance." Holden slid his gun along the door frame until the barrel was at eye level. "You know this guy or not?"

If either of them asked again, she might lunge for a gun. "No."

"Then you stay in here while I kill him," Holden said.

"Negative." Luke gave one shake of his head to match his clipped tone. "She doesn't move, but I want him alive. Need to know what's happening here and who's behind all this."

She knew. "I told you. It's Phil and he's—"

Luke ignored her. "The dot is moving."

And so were they. Holden and Luke slipped

into the hallway. Back to back they moved, guns up and bodies snapped stiff with tension.

Claire glanced down the hall toward the reception area. Everything in her screamed to run down the dark path and out the front door. She'd figure out her next step once she hit the street. But she didn't know the office building well enough to know where the mystery man could go and how he could get there. She couldn't risk a bullet in the back.

Plus, the idea of leaving Luke while danger swirled around them made her stomach heave. She had dragged him into this mess. She would get them both out. She just needed access to information and a way to hunt Phil down. A weasel like him couldn't hide for long. Sacrifice was not his style. She just hoped her last stand wouldn't be in a fake office with her furious ex nearby.

When shots rang out behind her, she forgot about everything except hitting the floor.

LUKE BIT DOWN on his lower lip as he eased his arm out of the sling. Pain screamed up his shoulder and pounded above his eyes.

Letting his muscles hang loose hurt more than he anticipated, but getting tangled up in the material was no way to fight.

Holden raised his eyebrows in question, but Luke waved him off. This was his fault. He'd brought Claire here into a sacred and private place and somehow dragged a stray behind them. He damn well knew better than to risk the agency's cover over a woman with a nonsense story. But it had always been that way with Claire. She walked in and his common sense skipped out.

The red dot moved along the inside wall of the conference room. In a few more steps, they'd be on opposite sides of three feet of shock-absorbing concrete. The construction of the office provided the advantage Luke needed. The barrier would stop a bullet, but their unwanted guest couldn't know that. That split second might give them the window they needed to get the jump on the guy.

Luke motioned for Holden to stop. As the red dot drew closer, Luke counted down on his fingers. The small movements sent new rounds of thumping up and down his arm. The pain might have stopped him, but the adrenaline racing through his veins proved stronger.

When the red dot came even with Luke's position in the hall, he didn't wait. There would never be a better chance. His third finger rose just as he crashed the uninjured side of his body into the thick wall and shouted. The goal was to make as much noise as possible. His teeth rattled when the hard surface refused to give at all.

The reaction inside the room was instantaneous. The cracks of gunshots reverberated through the quiet office. The man tried to shoot his way through, to take Luke out without ever facing him. The gunfire rang out in wild bursts, the impacts causing the concrete against Luke's shoulder to shake. With each round Luke tensed, waiting for the impromptu blockade to fail. When the wall shuddered but held, Luke knew the first part of his plan had worked.

But that was just the start.

Luke hit the doorway to the conference room a second after Holden. With the visitor concentrating on the sound outside, he failed to guard the room's only access. Holden entered with his gun raised. The first shot hit the man's thigh and he went down shooting. Gunfire exploded around the room. Holden dove for cover behind the conference table. Luke ducked back into the hallway. He peeked around the corner in time to see the attacker skim his gun along the floor, as if he planned to hit Holden from underneath through the legs of the chairs and table.

"Holden, roll!" Luke yelled over the rhythmic beats of gunfire and male grunts.

Surprise flashed across the visitor's face at the sound of Luke's voice. On the ground on his back with blood seeping into the carpet, the attacker tried to shimmy to the side and out of Luke's sight.

Luke wasn't having any of it. He ducked down and got off a shot just as the man fired at Holden. The attacker's shot went wild. Luke's hit straight on, causing the other man's body to jump. It hit him in the stomach, which meant Luke had to move before the man lost too much blood to be of any use to anyone.

"Got him." Luke jumped over to the injured man's side and kicked the weapon out of grabbing range.

Luke need not have rushed. The attacker curled on his side, gasping and gurgling as blood rushed out of him. "I need help here," Luke said.

"Coming." Holden dropped his weapon and hit his knees beside the man. "Man, how bad?"

"Very."

The injured man groaned as his eyes turned glassy. Luke flipped him onto his back. The low keening moan coming out of his throat reminded Luke of a death rattle. Unless help got here soon, the man's last minutes would consist of a series of long painful moments of bleeding out. Luke refused to let that happen.

"We've got to get him stabilized," Holden said as he pulled back the material and inspected the jagged wound.

"I should have aimed for his hand."

"There was no time. I, for one, am grateful you didn't hesitate." Holden balled his jacket and pressed it against the man's stomach to stop the flow of blood. "I can do this. Make the call."

Luke exhaled, trying to calm the unspent energy revving inside him. "Right."

He hit the red button on the other side of his watch. The emergency call would go out and people would come running. They'd never used the office warning system, never had to, but he had no choice now. The man on the floor, whoever he was, needed medical assistance.

And they would all need to protect their cover. That meant calling their boss, Rod Lehman, and preparing him for the questioning that was about to come down on him from above. The real work of Recovery Project might be top secret, but that didn't mean they could hide two bodies and clean up an office bloodbath without someone at Homeland asking a few questions. Luke couldn't imagine the bureaucratic crap storm that was about to hit them. And all because of Claire.

"Is he dead?" Her stunned voice rose over the commotion of Holden and Luke trying to keep the dying man alive.

"Not yet." Luke saw her huge eyes and trembling hands. He didn't need any more excitement or another chase. "Do not move from this room."

"I can't—"

Luke shot off the floor to stand in front of her. As gently as possible, he brushed a hand down her arm. "Listen to me." He waited until she tore her gaze away from the man on the floor and stared up at him, instead. "You are not safe alone."

"I know, but—"

"Get her out of here." Holden pressed down hard on the material as blood seeped out from underneath. "Neither of you can be here when everyone arrives."

"I don't have anywhere else to go."

Her soft voice spun through him, chipping away at the resistance he had built up against her over the past twenty-four months. "You're coming with me."

"It's not safe." She grabbed his sleeve. "I'm not safe to be around."

"We'll figure it out."

"Do whatever you're going to do now. You only have two minutes before the cars arrive." Holden's words rushed out between rough breaths.

"Sure you can handle this?" Luke asked.

"I'll take this guy." Holden glanced at Claire with a look most would describe as blank, but Luke knew to be one of festering anger. "You get her under control."

Sounded like an easy enough task, but Luke knew better. In the hours since they'd been reunited, he'd been shot at more than he had during an entire year in his current position. "We'll be at safe house two."

"Just watch your back."

Claire's mouth dropped open. "I wouldn't hurt him."

With their history, Luke found the comment pretty hollow. "I won't give you the chance." Not again.

"We don't know how many more are after her," Holden explained.

Maybe not, but Luke now doubted everything he knew about Phil Samson's supposed kidnapping and death. If someone really did murder the man, the least he could do was have the courtesy to stay dead and stop sending armed men after Claire. But that wasn't happening. Someone was gunning for her. Luke would bet it all led back to Phil.

The man ruined Luke's life once, looked

like he was trying to do it again. Money or not, Luke had no intention of losing this round.

Chapter Five

It took two hours for Claire to stop shaking. She stood at the kitchen sink and stared at her open hand. Her fingers trembled under the stream of cool water.

Luke stepped up beside her. He leaned his backside against the counter and faced her. "You okay?"

"No."

He glanced around the room. "I know the place is a bit less than what you're used to."

"Do you really think my problem is with the decor?"

"I gave up trying to understand you and what you thought a long time ago."

At first she thought he was itching for a fight. Then she really looked at him. Exhaustion pulled at his cheeks and mouth. From his eyes to his shoulders, everything drooped. "What about you?"

"I dunno. What about me?"

"You look ready to fall over."

"Apparently getting shot wreaks havoc with my stamina." He folded his arms over his chest.

"Was this your first time?"

He leaned in closer and whispered, "Are you fishing for information?"

She was desperate to gain some control over her situation. If all she could manage was an honest conversation about who and what Luke was, that was fine with her. "Yes."

"I'll pass."

So much for getting a little peace. "Either way, you should rest."

"Not going to happen."

She couldn't decide if he wanted to protect her or handcuff her. One thing was for certain, her hours of running and being scared witless convinced her the safest place to be was right by Luke's side. Injured or not, he was determined to find out what was happening to her. That gave them a united purpose. She could go and hide out on her own, but together they might meet their goal faster.

"I'm not going anywhere." For the first time in a long time she said it and meant it.

"You'll understand if I don't exactly trust your word about sticking around."

She didn't have the emotional energy for this battle now. More important, she knew he wasn't ready to listen. He would never understand that he'd unconsciously pushed her away. Yeah, she had made some terrible choices. She hurt him when she didn't even know that was possible. Stability, honesty. He couldn't see it, but Luke refused to give her either when he hid whole parts of his life from her.

She grew up with the burden of dangerous secrets. In another time she would have been called a bastard. That was what happened when a father set up two families simultaneously without enough money to support either. Claire and her mother, the second and expendable family, suffered. He was absent, lying, and loving another woman and child more than he ever loved Claire and her mom. When his double life was exposed, he had to make a choice. He threw Claire away.

Yeah, she knew about the things people

didn't say, knew that those never-spoken words could cut and destroy. She also knew what it was like to grow up poor and alone with everyone pointing and laughing. For her mother, cancer came as a welcome relief from the mocking. Claire learned a different lesson: rely only on yourself.

But rather than risk another argument, she switched topics. "Interesting house."

She had no idea where they were. Somewhere in Virginia, away from highways and the congestion of close-in D.C. Luke had driven for more than an hour, in the dark and fighting sleep as his eyes kept trying to close, until they pulled into a wooded area. No road. Just a gate that swung open upon command from his watch.

The one-story, one-bedroom house qualified more as a cabin than an actual residence. It was clean and stocked with food, so she couldn't complain. A long kitchen anchored the open living room on one end. The bedroom sat off to the right. Claire knew from looking that the only choice of sleeping arrangements was a king-size bed. That and the couch, which she planned to use tonight no matter how much Luke whined about her decision.

The rustic atmosphere and heavy furniture reminded her of hunting and fishing. She didn't associate either activity with Luke. "What is this place?"

"Somewhere safe."

"I don't see any art."

He smiled. "You mean antiques."

"What I mean is that it's time for you to tell me what you really do for a living, and skip the art talk or I'll quiz you on it."

"Does it really matter?" He turned around and poured a cup of coffee.

"I think so."

"Isn't the point that I can protect you?"

He still didn't get it, didn't understand how secrets festered until they destroyed everything. She learned that the hard way years ago. "Maybe I don't want someone throwing himself in front of me every ten seconds."

"You would have preferred I let the guy in the conference room shoot you?"

"Of course not."

"Then you must be talking about your husband."

Everything circled around to that. No matter how hard she tried to steer the conversation somewhere else, Luke brought it back. "My ex, and I rarely talk about him."

"Because?"

"I don't have anything good to say."

"Almost two years of marriage and not one good moment?" Luke took a long sip of his coffee. "I find that hard to believe."

"It doesn't work that way."

"Since I dodged the marriage bullet, why don't you explain to me what happens."

"It's about how those moments string together. For me, they never did." She tipped her head, letting her hair fall back. "I didn't love him. He didn't love me. A quick end was inevitable. I just never expected death and disaster."

Luke watched every move she made with a face pulled tight in confusion and something that looked like pain. "Then why, Claire? Why him?"

No. They needed to discuss this, but not when bullets were flying and unknown men nipped at their heels. "This isn't the right time."

"I've got nothing but time."

"That makes one of us." When she tried to move away, he grabbed her arm. She stared down at his long fingers. "You've picked up a nasty habit of manhandling women."

He dropped his hand. "I don't know how else to get your attention. You seem to spend most of your time running away from me."

"I'm here now."

"Why?"

"Because my ex-husband set me up."

"Not that." Luke shifted, inched closer, until his mouth hovered next to her cheek. "Why me? I'm not the only guy you know. Why show up in front of me, taunting me?"

Warm puffs of air brushed her skin. "I didn't know where else to go."

"Not good enough." The words sounded tough, but there was no heat behind them.

"I knew you were more than you claimed to be." She'd always known. His unwillingness to tell her was part of what broke them apart.

"Meaning?"

"I knew if you thought I was out there you'd follow me."

Their mouths nearly touched now. "I still don't get it."

"My thought was to lead you to Phil, prove he was alive and let you do the rest. You'd see that he was brought in, that my name was cleared."

Luke's head snapped back. "What makes you so sure of that?"

"Because while I never really knew you, I did understand you. You're one of the good guys. A rescuer at heart."

"I'm not sure the guy on the conference-room floor would agree with you."

"And whether you want to admit it or not, you're law enforcement and I needed a guy who could use a gun."

"So you wanted me for my weapon."

She laughed. Had to. "I'm not sure if there's some macho double meaning there, but yeah."

"That's good enough for now."

"There isn't anything else."

"That's where you're wrong, Claire. There's a lot between us. I don't like it any better than you do, but it's there beating with life and refusing to die."

"Luke, we shouldn't—"

"I know."

Then he was kissing her. Warm lips touched hers, sweeping and tasting until every muscle in her body turned to liquid. His fingers found the small of her back as one arm wrapped around her waist. His mouth slanted over hers again and again. The sensual assault hit her senses from every angle and seeped into every pore.

She wanted to forget all the fear and distrust, pain and betrayal. She wanted him. All he could give her and show her. A repeat of every second of sunshine they ever spent together.

"Yes," he whispered against her lips as his hand moved up to her cheek, then dived into her hair.

She fell into the kiss, returning his sure touches with her own. Hot breaths. Guttural moans. The memories of being with him came rushing back. Not that they had ever truly left. A woman didn't forget being overwhelmed by the joint pleasure of a man's mouth and hands.

Luke had that power over her.

Which was exactly why this moment had to stop. No matter how much her body begged for the familiar feel of him, this couldn't happen. Not now with the world upside down and so much left unsaid between them.

She turned her head to the side and fought for air. "Luke."

He took advantage of the angle, kissing a trail down her neck to the base of her throat. It would be so easy to throw her head back and let him lick and taste. Instead, she slipped her fingers into his hair and gave a gentle pull.

He broke off the kiss. With cloudy eyes and wet lips he stared at her. "What's wrong?"

"This. Us."

His chest rose and fell on hard breaths. He eased back, letting a few inches of air seep between them, but his hand didn't move from her body. "You're stopping?"

Everything she could see in his eyes—desire, confusion, a shocking sense of need—she felt deep inside. "We can't."

His brow knotted. "Because I got shot?"

She thought about using that excuse. "You seemed to be doing just fine with one hand."

"Then is it Phil?"

"It's because of *us*."

Luke dropped his arm until both hung lifeless by his sides. This time he did step back. He stood only a foot away, but his sudden coldness made it seem more like a mile. "Right."

"Luke, I just meant—"

He pointed at the other side of the room. "You take the bedroom."

The abrupt end left her reeling. "We need to talk about this. I want you to understand."

He rubbed his eyes. When he looked at her again, the sexual haze had disappeared. Back was the practical man who liked to bark orders. "We can either keep on doing what we're doing or we can go to bed. Separately. You don't get another option. Not after that lip action."

Her gaze traveled down his body. She could see his frustration in every line and muscle. The stiff shoulders and tight jaw, locked knees and an obvious erection pushing against his fly. Her abrupt halt left his body needing more. He was trying not to show it, not to let her know he felt anything, but the evidence was right there.

"I'm sorry," she whispered.

He dumped his coffee mug in the sink. "You say that a lot. Said it when you gave the ring back and walked away."

"You don't believe me?"

"As usual, Claire, I have no idea how to read you." He walked out of the kitchen area. "Be here when I get up tomorrow."

"Where else would I go?"

"I don't know, but next time I might disappoint you and not come, after all."

Chapter Six

Luke's arm still ached the next morning, but his body thrummed with a very different type of sensation. They stood outside the house Claire had once shared with Phil, and the only thing on Luke's mind was that burning kiss. Not the murder or her leaving. Just the kiss.

Two cold showers failed to knock the vision of Claire naked out of his head. Sure, things hadn't actually progressed that far, but they'd been well on the way. She'd put on the brakes and he respected that. But he didn't have to like it.

"I still don't understand why we're here." She paced the grass in the secluded area behind the three-story brick mansion.

"Nice place."

Her hands were in constant motion and her moves jerky and agitated. "Yeah, well, it's not my favorite."

"I think I saw this in a magazine once." To Luke it looked like a private prep school only with more security and a chandelier hanging in the window. The eight-foot black iron fence circling the property didn't exactly welcome people to stop by. Luke couldn't see Claire, young and vibrant, locked away in there.

"It's part of The Samson Family Trust," she said.

"What the hell is that?"

"A corporation Phil started with his brother, Steve. They own commercial and residential properties all across the metro area."

"Sounds like a lucrative arrangement."

"I wouldn't know."

That comment caught Luke's attention. "I don't pretend to be an expert, but shouldn't a man own a house with his wife?"

"Phil thought otherwise."

"Isn't one of the benefits of marrying the rich dude that you get the big house and fancy cars?" Luke tugged on a section of gate to test its strength. Even with diminished strength from the shooting, he still had one good hand and could tell the thickness of the metal. Unless there was a weakness somewhere or a blowtorch, no way did anyone break through those bars.

"I guess he was too busy setting me up for a murder charge."

"Well, there is that." Luke scanned the windows and second-floor balcony. No way could he hoist his body up there in his current condition. They'd have to go in through a door like normal people. "I want to look at the crime scene."

"No."

Her emphatic denial made him smile. "Excuse me?"

"The evidence is gone. It's bagged and sitting in a locker somewhere just waiting for me to go to trial."

"Feeling dramatic this morning?"

She sighed. "I don't know a calm way to face jail time."

"You have a point." He walked around the back of the house and away from the street.

Not that traffic was an issue. The property

sat on a secluded cul-de-sac in the exclusive suburb of McLean, Virginia. Country clubs and private schools littered the landscape. The yards stretched for acres and cost more than he'd earn in a lifetime of government work.

The area was home to dignitaries, congressmen, the CIA and Claire. No wonder she'd dumped him. It would be hard for anyone to say no to all this wealth and luxury. He lived in a two-bedroom condo off Capitol Hill small enough to fit into one of the property's four garages. Hardly competition for what Phil could give her.

It had always been that way. Luke, the son of an army colonel who picked up and moved his life every few years. Phil, the shiny millionaire who could buy her a house anywhere. Until he settled in with the Recovery Project and proposed to Claire, nothing had ever belonged to Luke. He lost the girl, but he saved the job he'd started around the same time. The job was the only thing that kept him sane when he saw her engagement notice in the paper less than a month after she dumped him.

Luke forced his mind back to the work. He

studied the ground, looking for obvious signs of breach. He heard the rustling behind him and then she appeared by his side.

"You could reassure me by telling me I'll never be convicted," she said in a dry tone.

"I need to see inside the house first."

"What are you looking for?"

"I'll know it when I find it."

"That's kind of trite."

He stopped. Without thinking he rubbed his bicep through his thin sweater. The sling was back at the safe house, but the nerves still burned.

"You came looking for me, not vice versa, remember?" he asked.

Her eyes closed on what looked suspiciously like a wave of pain. When she opened them again, the usual sparkle had dimmed. "I know."

Luke's instincts kicked in. She was saying something but not using any words to do it. "What?"

"Nothing."

"Are you trying to tell me something?"

"Yeah. I don't have the security codes anymore."

Luke wasn't sure what had just happened,

but he sensed he'd dodged some big emotional scene. He exhaled long and hard. "No worries. I have this." He held up a security card.

"The key to your office?"

"A little 'get in free' insurance."

When they reached the back gate, Luke slid the card into place, then hooked a cable from one end of it to his watch. Numbers and letters flashed on the small screen.

Her toe began to tap against the thick grass. "Still insisting you don't work for the FBI?"

"The FBI doesn't have anything this cool." The lock clicked as the gate opened. "And we're in."

"Won't the police be here?"

"Adam's been watching the place. No one is here but us." Luke checked and double-checked before dragging Claire with him. "Which is why we picked daytime. Don't have to worry about turning on lights and tipping off a neighbor, though I now get that someone would need a telescope to see in here."

"There are cameras everywhere inside and outside."

"They still on?"

She glanced at the brick patio just inside the gate but didn't move closer. "How would I know?"

"You did live here once, right?"

"Phil's brother Steve moved me out the same night I was at the police station being interrogated for seven hours."

"Why didn't they arrest you then?"

"Not enough evidence. They were waiting for the forensics to come back."

"So you ran."

"Wouldn't you?"

"I wouldn't have married Phil in the first place." Luke took the first steps. He walked across the patio toward the set of French doors. When he realized he was alone, he glanced over his shoulder. "You coming?"

"Depends. Are you ready to stop with the digs about Phil?"

"Not quite yet." When she made that face, the one that telegraphed an I'm-about-to-explode urgency, Luke changed tactics. "I need you with me in there."

"It's not easy to walk back in there after all that's happened. After my last trip here."

Ah, there it was. This was about the divorce

and memories from the last time she walked through the place.

Luke thought about kicking his own ass over his insensitivity. "I'm not trying to torture you. I really do need someone with inside knowledge of this place. That's you."

She waved her hand in front of her. "Forget it. It doesn't matter."

"Yeah, it does. But nothing's going to happen to you in there. I won't let it."

CLAIRE BELIEVED HIM. And when Luke held out his hand, she didn't balk. She grabbed on and held tight. Walking through the rooms, seeing the bloodstain, knowing now that it was all fake, started a headache pounding in her temples.

But if this was what it took to get Luke to believe her story, then she'd do it. "Let's go."

"That's my girl."

They walked fast and low across the open outside area, around the pool and barbecue pit. When they hit the back door, Luke repeated his covert operative skills. Two seconds later, she stepped into the family room of what was never really her house.

"You entered where that night?" he asked.

She dropped his hand and crossed the room, walking down the hall until they hit the marble two-story foyer.

Luke stared up at the winding staircase. "Damn, that's impressive."

It had all wowed her once. The intricate carvings and gentle slope of the curves. Now all she saw was another reminder of Phil's over-the-top spending on things that didn't matter.

She stood with her back against the double doors leading to the front yard. "I parked in the driveway and came in right here."

"And then you went up the stairs without poking around down here."

"Because I heard noises up there. Yes."

Luke jogged up a few steps and then turned around to face her. "I know this stinks, but I need you to come up with me."

"Why?"

He dropped his gun to his side.

She wasn't even sure when he drew it.

"First," he said, "I'm betting there's more than one bedroom up there, so I might need some guidance to pick the right one." When she started to talk, he raised his hand to cut her off. "And second, I need to see you at the scene."

"That sounds ghoulish."

"The theory is that you dragged a man almost twice your size down these stairs and out of this house—all without getting more than a few drops of blood on the marble, I might add—and then hid him in a place where the police and all their dogs and equipment couldn't find him."

She was afraid to hope, but some pressure was lifted from her chest. "Sounds ridiculous, doesn't it?"

"Looking at the size of this house, I'm thinking that it's impossible, but I want to be sure."

She closed her eyes and let a wave of relief crash over her. She didn't have anyone. All her supposed friends had abandoned her, choosing to chase the money and side with Phil. Steve screamed at her, nearly inconsolable with grief. And her family was long gone. That left…no one to root for her.

"Thank you," she whispered.

"For what?"

"Believing."

He stared at her for an extra beat before nodding his head. "Upstairs."

THE NEXT HOUR moved in slow motion. The bloodstain still marked the carpet. Luke made her wait in the hallway while he walked around the former master suite. He said something about her leaving additional genetic material behind, which probably explained why gloves appeared out of his pocket.

Luke finally looked up. "We're done."

"What does that mean?"

"Unless you threw Phil out the window, and I'm thinking there would be a sign of that, I can't see how the timeline can work. The prosecutor must be hoping he has enough other evidence to overcome that flaw, or that science will provide an answer."

"I didn't do it."

He stripped off the gloves and shoved them in his back pocket. "Yeah, it looks that way. The press has pointed out the timeline problem. The prosecutor says there's an explanation but isn't sharing. I'm guessing the real answer is that they haven't come up with a reasonable story just yet."

She thought about throwing herself into his arms, but his watch started beeping. "What's that?"

"The alarm on my car." Luke joined her in the hallway and showed her his arm. "Recognize this guy?"

"You have a camera in your car?"

"Claire." Luke snapped his fingers. "Focus."

She shook her head to clear out everything and concentrate. A man with dark hair and dark clothes slipped around the side of the car. She couldn't make out his face, couldn't see what he was doing, but now it looked as if he was on his knees under the automobile.

"He's probably planting a tracking device." Luke swore to let her know what he thought about the idea.

"Who is it?"

"Someone who knows you're with me."

"Phil would hate that." The words slipped out before she could stop them.

Luke scoffed. "Why? He won you."

No, he didn't. Claire knew that as well as Phil did. "I'm not a prize to be fought over."

"Is that the point you're going with here? That I said something offensive? Seems to me my assessment was pretty accurate despite my choice of words."

"No." She exhaled, knowing this was the wrong thing to say, but she was going to do it, anyway. "Phil would hate to see me with you because he thought I never got over you."

Luke's eyebrows rose. "Paranoid guy."

"And smart, too."

Luke's eyes narrowed. "What are you saying?"

"Exactly what you think."

"Claire—"

She jumped ahead before he could dissect her words and drag them into a conversation neither of them wanted. "So what does it mean that someone else is sneaking around the house?"

He opened his mouth to say something, but then closed it again. It took another second for him to speak. "We need another way out of here. They're watching the house."

"You think someone followed us here." The idea made the contents in her stomach roll. It seemed that Phil knew every move she made. The blow to her privacy left her feeling raw.

"I know they did." Luke pointed at the watch. The mystery man disappeared off screen as he headed toward the mansion. "I'm betting he has a key and he'll know which room to search first."

"There's a back staircase we can use."

Luke started shaking his head before she finished the suggestion. "No good. He could have a partner waiting there. We need something less obvious."

"I can't fly, so the windows are out."

"I was hoping a big place like this might have a few secret entrances, that sort of thing."

"If it does, Phil never shared them with me." She tensed when the security system chirped. "He's in."

"Where's the balcony?"

Her mind refused to function. "What?"

"The one I could see from the backyard. Where is it?"

The blueprints snapped into place in her mind. She walked as fast and as quietly as possible into the sitting room to the left of the bedroom. The balcony doors were against the back wall.

Luke didn't waste any time explaining his plan. He turned the lock. The sound of the soft click bounced off the walls. Claire couldn't remember the last time she heard a noise so loud.

As if reading her mind, Luke shook his head. "Imagination."

"Right."

He pushed his gun into her hand. "Know how to use this?"

The cold metal burned her fingers. "You need it."

"I have another. Here." He motioned for her to step out onto the balcony. "Anyone but me comes out here, you scream and shoot. Got it?"

Her pulse danced a crazy beat. "Luke, stay with me."

"Right now we have surprise on our side."

Before she could argue, he shut the door, leaving her alone outside. He stepped into the connecting closet.

And then they waited.

She tried to wait over to the side, just in

case the sun cast a shadow in the glass. From her position she could watch the closet. Luke didn't peek out. Nothing moved. She couldn't hear anything but the knocking of her own heart.

Minutes ticked by with a dedicated slowness that made her itch to burst through the doors and run down the stairs to freedom. Every second of standing out there, exposed and hanging on to the railing, passed like a week. Just when she decided to give up and go inside to grab Luke, a floorboard creaked just on the other side of the wall from where she stood.

Her body switched into shut-down mode. Air didn't flow. Her muscles froze. She stood as still as possible, trying not to breathe.

The outline of a male appeared in the window and close enough for her to see the sleeve of his coat. She had to bite down on her lower lip to keep from screaming in surprise. The gun in her hand started to shake. When her vision started to blur, she blinked to clear it again.

Just as the man turned toward her hiding place, a shout of fury cut through the room.

Luke flew out of the closet and launched his body at the other man. Guns clattered to the floor. One spun across the hardwood and landed under the bed as the men fell to the floor. Legs and arms were everywhere, fighting and punching. The men rolled, stopping only when they slammed into the chest of drawers. Then they started the free-for-all again.

Claire stepped inside. "Luke!" She aimed her gun but couldn't get off a decent shot, not with her lack of skill. One wrong move and she could fire right into the back of Luke's head.

Luke yelled in pain when the other man pressed his thumb right into the gunshot wound. It was as if the guy knew where to push and how to inflict the most damage. Luke landed a punch to the man's throat and managed to shift away from the grinding grip. Luke pulled back, rising to his knees, his injured arm hanging from his side like it was no longer attached. Blood dripped from under his sweater and down the back of his hand.

Now that the man knew Luke's weakness,

he went for it again. Through grunts and swearing, Luke lifted his knee and popped the man in the groin. The guy dropped on his side. As he writhed on the floor, Luke scrambled on his stomach a few feet away. He snatched his gun from under the edge of the bed just as the other man landed a punch to the back of Luke's knee.

Eyes bulging, Luke kicked out, catching the man across the jaw. The guy's head snapped back as his eyes rolled and his head hit the floor. The shouting gave way to dead silence. With his arms thrown out to the side and mouth hanging open, the guy didn't move.

Claire stood over him with the gun just to be sure. "Is he dead?"

Luke flopped back against the bed. He covered his injury with his hand as he breathed in heavy pants. "It amazes me how you say that as if it doesn't matter."

"He was trying to kill you." As far as she was concerned that meant the guy deserved whatever he got, even if it was an early grave.

"No kidding."

"Do we call the police?"

"Only if you want to be arrested." Luke struggled to his feet.

She rushed over to help him, sliding her shoulder under his armpit for balance. "That was impressive."

"He knew about the gunshot wound. Knew right where to take me. That means someone else was following the guy in the alley. We have a group working together, which is not good." After a few steps Luke stopped.

"We'll worry about that later."

"I'm pretty ticked off about it right now."

"You okay?"

"Will be." He shook off her assistance. After a few more deep breaths he stood up straight, wincing and grumbling with every move.

Claire refused to be offended. It was clear this show of machismo was more about proving to himself that he was fine than anything else. A guy like Luke needed to know he was in charge, so she let him have that moment.

She looked around for a rope or something to use as a tie in case the guy on the floor woke up swinging. Nothing. Someone had cleaned the place out except for the furniture on the floor and paintings on the wall. No knickknacks. No clothing, not even hers. Steve sure did erase her presence in a hurry.

"We've got to get out of here." Luke clicked a button on his watch.

"We're not going to bring him in? Question him?"

"No way to do that since I don't know what he did to my car and I can't exactly carry him to the bus stop."

She stared down at the guy. Other than a small lift of his chest, he didn't even twitch. "But what if he talks?"

"He won't. He's not supposed to be here, either, remember?" Luke crouched down and searched through the man's pockets. He held up a key. "This is all he has on him."

"Travels light."

She watched as Luke scooped up the man's gun with two fingers and dropped it on the bed. With a flick of his wrist, the pillow came out of its case and the gun went in.

"I'll call it in, have my guys try to round him up and tow my car just to be safe," Luke said. "Tell them to check the security tapes and erase them while they're at it so no one sees you."

"Thanks."

"We need to figure out why these guys keep coming, and if Phil is sending them, just where he's hiding."

"Think this one will say anything more than the guy who broke into your office did?"

"They'll crack eventually. Once they realize the help and money aren't coming, they'll turn. They just need time."

She wanted to ask if the office attacker had been arrested, but a tiny voice in her brain told her not to. Luke and his buddies didn't work through regular channels, which meant the men they captured weren't going to be sitting in jail cells waiting to meet with their court-appointed attorneys.

"And, Claire?"

Something about the lightness in Luke's voice had her glancing up at him. "Yeah?"

"I still don't work for the FBI."

Chapter Seven

"We've got trouble." Holden delivered his observation while pacing back and forth in front of the small refrigerator in the safe house.

"You mean more trouble." Luke sat propped up on the couch with an ice pack plastered to his wound. The thing thumped like a son of a bitch thanks to the unwanted wrestling at the mansion. The bleeding had finally tapered off, but not until Adam came over and did more stitching.

Holden grabbed a beer and then plunked on the couch by Luke's feet. "The forensics in Phil's case point to Claire."

"Not possible."

"You sure that's your head talking and not some other part of you?"

"I saw the house, the supposed murder

scene. No way could she have managed what the prosecution says she did. I'm telling you that man walked out of there very much alive."

Holden stretched his arm across the back of the sofa. "You think she's being set up."

"There's no other story that makes sense."

Holden nodded. "I agree."

"Thank heaven for smart men." Claire walked into the room wearing the slim T-shirt and pajama pants Holden had delivered. She had scrubbed her face clean and pulled her hair up in a ponytail.

She managed to look both fresh and strong. The combination proved irresistible to Luke. Looking at her now, he wondered how he ever let her walk out on him. Why he didn't tamp down his ego and rush after her when she started talking about needing more than he could give.

"We figure things out eventually," Holden said.

"Not bad for art dealers."

"Antiques." Holden and Luke corrected her at the same time.

"The gadgets I saw today, those kicking

and slicing moves?" She imitated the fighting as she spoke. "That ain't like any museum curator I've ever seen."

Luke knew she deserved an explanation. After everything they'd been through over the past day, she was entitled. "We find people for a living."

"Luke." Holden said his friend's name like a warning.

"She's watched me track down attackers and fight. She's not stupid." Luke had fought telling her everything for so long that he was surprised at how right it felt to just spill it. "We're not FBI. We're much better."

"But you're with the government."

"Sort of."

"I'm not sure how one is 'sort of' a government agent."

"When one works undercover at a place with few rules."

A huge smile burst across her lips. It was the kind of pure joy that could feed him forever.

"Now was that so hard to tell me?" she asked in a saucy tone.

"Yes," Holden mumbled. "And it's top secret, so not a word to anyone. You think the boneheads chasing you now are a problem? Imagine having me on your tail if you open your mouth."

She smiled over the threats. "I got it."

Holden plowed on. "You talk and we'll deny. We have an entire backstory that will refute anything you have to say. That is, if anyone can find you."

"That's enough." Luke figured his friend had made the point. Claire didn't look scared. If anything she looked excited at having been let in on the big secret.

Her reaction made him wish he could have told her back then. But he'd been new and had understood that the rules didn't bend. He didn't want to blow his assignment or get kicked out during the probationary period. Mostly, he'd thought she should accept his word and leave the rest. Now he wasn't so sure things were ever that absolute when it came to trust.

She sat on the floor in front of them and crossed her legs in the way only women can do. "Your secret is safe."

"You." Holden pointed at Luke. "Shut up before I use some of Adam's thread and sew your mouth closed."

Luke lifted his hands in mock surrender. "Yes, boss."

Claire's eyes grew wide. "Holden is in charge?"

"No."

"I should be," Holden said at the same time.

"So no one is talking, the rope around Claire's neck is tightening, and my real boss is tired of cleaning up bodies after me." Luke leaned back. "Does that sum up your message for today?"

"That and the fact someone is digging around in your financial and employment records," Holden said.

Claire's smile fell flat. "What?"

"Even broke into Luke's house and had a look around."

Luke wasn't happy with that news, but he wasn't surprised, either. Clearly whoever wanted Claire knew she was with him. It was only a matter of time before he became a target. "Anything missing in my condo?"

Holden tapped his beer bottle against his knee. "Not that I could see."

"Then it's no big deal. I don't keep work

stuff there or anything that could trace back to the office." When Luke saw the rage boiling behind Claire's eyes, he rushed to soothe her. "We have all sorts of bells that go off when this sort of thing happens. If anything, it might give the computer experts in the office a way to track down the people at the top of this mess."

"And there's one more thing." Holden took a long swig of beer as if prolonging the anticipation. "Steve Samson, Phil's brother."

"What about him?" she asked.

"He wants to talk to Luke."

Claire looked appalled at the idea. The scrunched-up nose and flat mouth gave her away. "For God's sake, why?"

"He knows you two had a past relationship. He wants to know if Luke knows anything about where you are and where you might be going."

Luke saw the news as an opportunity. "Interesting."

"Don't you mean annoying?" Holden asked.

"It opens a door."

Claire looked back and forth between Luke and Holden, the frown on her face deepening by the second. "Can I have the non-spy translation of that sentence please?"

"While Steve is sizing me up, I can do the same to him."

Holden balanced his bottle against his leg. "You think he's involved in all of this?"

"If Phil is dead—"

"He's not," Claire said in a tone that suggested no one disagree with her.

"Humor me." Luke waited until Claire stopped fidgeting to continue. "If Phil is gone, then who would be the one person to benefit? I'm guessing that would be his brother, who is also business partner in several lucrative property corporations."

"Steve." She shook her head. "But we always got along."

"I don't remember him supporting you in the divorce or after the police showed up." And Luke knew because he followed the news with an obsession that scared the hell out of him. Even though she had walked out, even though he hated her, seeing her scared and shaken as the police dragged her in for questioning was a vision that Luke could never shake out of his head.

"That's different."

"Is it?" Luke asked.

Her shoulders slumped. "I hate the Samson family."

"That makes two of us."

IT TOOK ANOTHER two hours to kick Holden out of the house and get Claire to stop spouting off about everything she'd ever heard or known about Steve. She was trying to help, but once she got turned on to a subject, it proved near impossible to turn her off again.

With the lights out and his head balanced on the pillows on the couch, Luke was ready for the sweet oblivion of sleep. He had skipped the serious painkillers in favor of a second beer and an aspirin.

"Luke?" Claire's soft voice slid through the room.

He sat up fast enough to wrench his shoulder…again. He bit back a groan. "What's wrong?"

"I think you should take the bed."

He'd been thinking about the mattress and her on it for longer than he wanted to admit.

"I'm fine," he said in a voice rubbed raw from wanting her.

"You're not."

"Nothing that a few hours of rest won't cure."

"I'd rather you skip the rest and share the bed with me."

In the darkness he couldn't see her face, couldn't read her motives. The only thing that was clear was the glow of the short white nightgown she now wore and the outline of her body underneath.

This sounded like an offer, but he'd been down that road with her before and didn't plan to take that turn again. "I'm comfortable here."

Which was a damn lie.

He heard the shuffle of bare feet against the floor. Then she was on her knees beside the couch. Her hair spilled off her shoulders and onto his bare shoulder. "I want you with me."

He shut his eyes and struggled for control. "Claire, I'm not really up for a night of cold showers."

"You aren't understanding me."

Every muscle in his body tensed. "I'm trying."

"Then listen."

"Just say what you want."

"Sleep with me." And she didn't mean sleep. This time the message got through. Probably had a lot to do with the way she pressed her palm against his stomach.

"Be sure."

"I am."

There were a thousand reasons to say no. He ignored every last one of them. "Then yes."

He tried to cool the churning inside him and not run into the other room to get started. Instead, he threw back the covers and sat up nice and slow, giving her plenty of time to change her mind and take off. That was her specialty, after all.

She stood up and held out her hand to him. "Ready?"

No. He wasn't sure he'd ever be ready for this. All those fantasies about pushing her away crumbled under the weight of his need and the brush of her fingers down his cheek.

"I'll be gentle with you," she whispered against the back of his hand right before she placed a kiss there.

He could hear the smile in her voice. He

almost laughed at the thought. When they'd come together in the past, it was fiery and passionate, a wreck-the-bed-and-roll-on-the-floor type of thing. They'd acted as if every minute could be their last. Eventually it was.

He waited until they crossed the threshold to the bedroom to pull her into his arms and match his lips with hers. Over and over he pressed until the feel of her consumed him.

The kissing ignited something deep inside him. This part always felt so right. And those moments right before he entered her tortured him as much this time as they did before. The waiting and wanting, he could barely contain it.

She slid the straps of her nightgown off her shoulders and let the light material slip to the floor. Naked and ready, not an ounce of shame as she wound her arms around his neck and pulled him closer. Her bare breasts rubbed against his chest and he was lost. Only a flash of common sense saved him from being reckless.

"Wait," he said as he broke off the kiss. "Protection."

She nibbled on his neck. "On the bed."

"Holden brought condoms?"

"Apparently he's a *very* good friend." She pushed Luke down until his butt balanced on the edge of the mattress.

When she straddled his lap, he forgot about everything else. All his doubts and concerns slipped away. All that mattered was her.

His mouth moved over hers as their hands went exploring. His back hit the bed and he rolled them over, careful not to put any pressure on his weak shoulder.

"No." She shoved against his chest. "Let me."

The words refused to compute in his head. It wasn't until she turned him onto his back again and stripped off his boxer briefs that he understood. She would be in charge tonight. He wouldn't have to worry about his weak arm because she would guide them through.

A rip echoed through the quiet room and Luke knew what was next. Her hand covered him, putting on the protection and bringing him to a fullness that had his back arching off the comforter.

"Claire—"

"Now, Luke." Then she slid down over him.

His body shuddered when she started to move. The steady rhythm pounded through every part of him. Then she shifted positions and he lost the ability to breathe.

Chapter Eight

Claire stared at the laptop screen and waited for something interesting to happen. If someone had told her a month ago that she'd be sitting in a safe house watching Luke have a chat with her former brother-in-law, she would have found the nearest mental-health professional for a prescription pad.

"How did you manage to get a camera in the coffee shop?" she asked Holden. If he was going to stay stapled to her side while Luke was gone, the least the guy could do was answer a question or two.

"There are cameras everywhere. It's a simple matter of tapping into them."

"Adam?"

Holden flipped a chair around and sat down next to her. "It's his specialty."

"Adam has computers. Luke has guns. You're, what, head of sarcasm?"

"Tactics and strategy."

"Aren't those the same thing?"

"No."

She gave in to an eye roll. "Okay, but wouldn't it have made more sense to use your office downtown for this meeting, instead of some random Georgetown restaurant? You would have had more control. Seems to me you guys are all about control."

"It's been compromised."

She tapped her fingers against the table. "Because of me."

"Yes."

The plan seemed so simple a few days ago. Now everything was twisted. Luke got hurt and they ended up in bed. She had no idea how to pull back and reassess.

"Sorry," she murmured.

"You don't sound it."

She pointed at Luke's image. "I still don't understand what Luke hopes to accomplish with this meeting."

He sat slumped over a cup of coffee. The cell phone on the table beside him was actually a speaker so they could hear and record every word. So far, the men had only managed polite introductions. At this rate, she'd be on death row before Luke ate his muffin.

"Information." Holden said the word and then let it sit there.

"Are you just throwing out words, or is that supposed to mean something?"

"Steve's pretty sure you killed his baby brother. He's been all over the news calling for your arrest. It's not exactly a stretch to think that he's angry enough to send someone, or a bunch or someones, after you." Holden turned up the volume.

She figured he hoped to drown out her questions. Not like she was going to let that happen. "Phil is at the bottom of this."

"I know you think that."

"He's framing me."

Holden folded his arms over the top of his chair and leaned down. "See, that's the part I don't quite get. I know you've got Luke staking his reputation and job on this…"

The allegation rumbled through her. "That's not true."

"Sex will do that to a man, but I don't understand what *Phil* gains. It's easier to cut you a small slice and get rid of you through a nasty divorce, especially since he has the upper hand in public opinion."

"You sound like my lawyer."

"So why go through the big scene? Why walk away from everything?"

She had turned that question over in her head a thousand times, dissecting it and breaking down the facts. The logic of Phil's actions eluded her. If he wanted to prove he hated her, he did that when he filed the paperwork accusing her of infidelity, a charge he knew wasn't true.

"He must be hiding something." It was the only explanation that made sense.

"I combed through the financial records. I'm not an expert and couldn't get very deep, but on the surface the company looks solid. Times are rough everywhere, but he's got some cash flow. Enough to pay the bills and keep everything afloat. Certainly shoveled a lot of money in his attorney's direction to get rid of you."

"Thanks for the reminder."

"So why dump it all? Why is setting you up so important?"

A loud thumping caught her attention. She realized the drumming of her fingers grew louder the more frustrated she became.

She flattened her palms against the table. "I don't know."

"Think, Claire. There's got to be something."

Holden's sharp tone surprised her. "You believe I'm holding out on you? I don't gain anything by doing that."

"You get Luke back."

"That's not what this is."

"I have eyes. I know you still want him."

Holden had been waiting to drop that little insight. She could tell by the way he froze as if waiting for a denial. Well, she wasn't going to let him think he won on that point. "This is about clearing my name."

Holden studied her as if he was memorizing her reaction and analyzing it in some internal computer. At last he nodded. "I hope for your sake that Luke can weasel something out of this little rodent."

"Or what?"

"Just hope he can."

LUKE TRIED to hide his contempt for the forty-something, balding millionaire sitting across from him. Maybe if Steve hadn't driven up in a car that cost as much as Luke's condo, they could have found some common ground. But between the expensive business suit and general air of disgust for the chosen rendezvous spot as reflected in his sour look, Steve Samson made his position quite clear. He viewed himself as above it all. This was a task he had to perform. It was less about real concern than it was about familial duty.

Luke found Steve's oversize ego laughable. The man came off as the older, less attractive, less polished Samson brother. Extra pounds sat around his middle and disdain dripped off him. But the reality was simple. In a competition with Phil on style and public opinion, Steve lost.

In the ultimate insult, Phil was even blessed with a full head of hair and a chin that didn't dissolve into the rolls on his neck. It had to suck to be outshone so brightly.

"I know this is a sensitive topic." Steve

used a napkin to wipe the crumbs off the table and onto the floor.

"How so?"

"You have a…history, shall we say, with Claire."

Luke glanced around the empty shop. No one would notice or complain if he punched Steve in the face. If the conversation kept going like this, that was a significant possibility.

"We were engaged."

"Yes, that's right." Steve leaned his elbows against the table before sitting up straight again and brushing off his sleeves.

"And she picked your brother over me. So?"

Saying the words made Luke bite the inside of his cheek. His job was to pretend to give a crap about what Steve had to say. To suck it up and play along. Still, talking about Claire with a family member who welcomed her, then discarded her made Luke want to flip the table over.

"In light of the circumstances I would think you'd be grateful."

"For?"

"Being left behind."

Luke hated this guy more with each passing second. "Interesting choice of words."

"My brother is dead. You could be, as well, if you had been Claire's true target." Steve made the statement with a detachment that left Luke cold.

Luke didn't have a sibling. He had never really known his mother. She'd skipped out of the military lifestyle long before he was old enough to become attached to her. But he had his dad. They moved and shuffled, but belonged to each other. When his dad died, Luke lost something. A piece of him broke off inside. Crumbled. Yet Steve sat there thinking his baby brother was gone and talking about it with all the emotion one would normally reserve for reading the sports page.

"Has Phil's death been confirmed?"

"There isn't another explanation." Steve touched the top of Luke's phone. "Why, if Claire has nothing to hide, is she running?"

Luke fought the urge to pull his cell out of reach. "Why are you asking me?"

"I thought it might be possible that you'd spoken with her." Steve's eyes gleamed.

The guy reminded Luke of a trapped

animal. A feral one. "We didn't exactly break up on good terms."

"Of course, but I thought it conceivable that..." Steve shot Luke a man-to-man look, one that suggested a deeper familiarity than they would ever share. "Well, please understand that how you lead your private life is not my concern."

Luke felt the heat rise in his cheeks. "I think we can agree on that much."

"There was some suggestion that Claire might have continued to see you after she married my brother." Steve held up a hand. "I'm not judging. She is a beautiful woman. There's something about her that worms its way into a man's life before he can build a wall to keep her out."

"Ouch."

"Certainly you agree with my assessment of Claire, what with the way she discarded you. Unless, of course, the rumors are true and she never did."

Hearing this man say her name made Luke's hands ball into fists. "Who's been suggesting that?"

"That's not important."

"It is to me."

"My point is that after all of her maneuvering and lies, you might be of a mind to tell me where she is."

"Uh-huh."

"If so, I might be in a position to help you in return."

"You're talking money." Luke was surprised it took Steve this long to whip out the checkbook and compare balances.

"You strike me as a practical man, Luke Hathaway."

"True."

"And I am someone who appreciates information. I think we could make our objectives work together, don't you?"

Only if your objective has something to do with being punched in the face. "I'd think with all of your resources, Steve, you would have been able to track down one woman by now."

"She is well financed."

There was news. From what he could tell Claire didn't have enough cash to buy a pair of socks. "I thought she walked out of the marriage without anything."

"There is some information the public doesn't know."

A familiar rumbling started deep in Luke's gut. The sensation rose inside him whenever he hovered on those last few steps before gaining the information he needed. "Such as?"

"This is confidential, you understand."

Like he would ever share a confidence with this guy. "Understood."

"Money is missing."

"From?"

Steve glanced around and then leaned in as if sharing a trade secret. "This is the difficult part. You see, in addition to a family trust, Phil and I run a very successful commercial real-estate-development company. We're responsible for most of the new construction you see in the Maryland suburbs. We develop—"

Enough with the advertisement. "What does this have to do with Claire?"

"The company employs over four hundred people. People with pension funds that are now missing."

Luke had not seen that allegation coming. He didn't believe it one bit, but he gave Steve credit for dropping it at just the right moment. "You're saying Claire stole money out of office accounts without anyone knowing it?"

"Yes."

"Did she even work there?"

"She is a very enterprising young woman. Convinced Phil to discuss vital business facts with her, shared the paperwork. That sort of thing."

"And somehow she wrote a big business check to herself without anyone seeing?"

"She has those skills. I would venture to say if Phil had understood her background before they got married..." Steve sat back in his chair. Made quite a scene of pretending to be buddies, as he shook his head. "Well, let's just say it's unlikely we would be in this position."

"Her background?"

"Her father was a con man. Look how she caught Phil."

Luke wasn't sure what bits of information grew out of a truth, but he suspected the one about Claire's father did. "Why isn't the news about the theft all over the press?"

"We're holding back those pieces, hoping

to flush Claire out. It is possible, at this point, that some of the money can be recovered. We need to tread carefully for the sake of our employees."

"And you think she's still in town?"

"I know she is. There have been sightings."

And shootings. In Luke's mind, the only thing missing at this point was a car chase. "Have you checked the house?"

"Phil is the owner of several properties. The only one that's open and not being watched is the family horse farm out in Loudon County."

"She doesn't strike me as the farm-girl type."

"Except for staff, no one else goes there. It's actually a fairly recent purchase. Phil bought it for Claire when they got married. As a surprise he had it remodeled, and that's only recently been completed."

"Claire owns a farmhouse."

Steve scoffed. "Well, no. The Samson family owns it. I doubt she could even find it. Once Phil suspected there was a problem in the marriage and with Claire's honesty, he took great pains to make sure she never knew of the property except as a business investment."

"So he bought her a house and then didn't tell her about it." Yeah, that made about as much sense as everything else Steve was saying. Luke just wondered how much more he had to hear.

"To my knowledge he never took Claire there or let it be known that it was to be her legacy. We quietly folded it into the business. You see, Phil didn't trust his wife."

"Obviously."

"Turns out he was right to be troubled."

"Sounds like it, but look, I can't help you. I cut my ties with her a long time ago."

"All I am asking is that you be aware. If she does come to you, please contact me." Steve reached into his jacket and pulled out a business card. He slid it across the table. "My deal is always open."

"Good to know."

HOLDEN CLEARED his throat. "You can let go of my arm now."

Claire eased her fingernails out of his skin.

She didn't even know she had him in a death grip until he mentioned it. "I'm sorry."

"I could be wrong, but I think Steve doesn't like you."

She pushed the chair back, letting it squeak against the wood floor. "Because he accuses me of theft and low morals?"

"Yeah, that's about where I sensed the dislike."

"I had dinner with that man every week." She pointed at the empty screen. "He was decent to my face and…and…"

"I get it."

"Do you think he believes that garbage?"

"I think he trusts his brother."

She snorted. "So did I."

"Right now we have bigger problems." Holden tapped on the keys.

"What?"

"Someone, probably someone who took Steve up on his big money offer, is following Luke."

The laptop switched to a street scene. Claire could see Luke's dark sedan. When Holden split the image, she saw the second car. "What are we going to do?"

"Wait an extra half hour for Luke to get back while he loses the clown."

"But he—"

"Have a little faith, Claire."

That's the one thing of which she'd always had a very low supply. "I do."

Holden smiled. "Nah, not yet. But you'll learn."

Chapter Nine

The next morning Luke stood by his car and stared down at the map of Loudon County spread out on his hood. From Adam's digging through court records and corporate shell companies, they knew the top-secret Samson property sat a mile to the west.

Luke knew he wanted to get in there and poke around. Putting an end to this mess for Claire moved farther out of reach the more they worked. The evidence kept stacking up against her. Much more and it would fall right on top of her.

But that wasn't what ate at Luke on this cloudy fall morning. A day later and he still hadn't brushed off the stench of sitting at a table with Steve. The guy's words lingered. Not that Luke believed the garbage about

Claire stealing pension funds. He didn't need Adam to trace that one. If money was missing, she was not the one to blame. He refused to believe her faults extended to embezzlement.

Besides that, the facts just didn't fit. If she had that kind of cash, counting into the millions, and really had no compunction about taking what wasn't hers, then she'd be gone. Her integrity wouldn't have forced her to stay. Sticking around for the sole purpose of driving him nuts and taking another tumble between the sheets didn't make any sense. No, Claire didn't take the money.

That left Phil or Steve. Luke hoped that something in this house would point to one of them. Finding Phil alive and kicking back by the fireplace would do it. With that information, Luke could go to the police and prosecutor. Until then, he had a bunch of theories and a bullet wound and little else to prove Claire's innocence.

"Why are you frowning?" Claire asked as she fought with the cool breeze to hold down the edge of the map.

"I still don't like this. You being here. It feels wrong."

"It's always nice to spend some quality time together. Happy to know you appreciate it."

"You know what I mean. This is dangerous."

"Too scary for the little lady?" She skimmed her fingers over the red circle outlining the acres the Samson family owned. "Get over the macho garbage. This was your plan, if you recall."

His temper flared to life, licking at the inside of his skull and begging to get out. "To come out here, yeah. But my scenario had you back at the safe house listening to the radio—"

"Like that would happen."

"—while we carried out the surveillance."

She stared him down even though she had to lift her chin to do it. With hands on her hips and the skin of her cheeks pulled tight in anger, she treated him to a tsk-tsk sound.

"You know I'm right," he fired off before she could launch into whatever diatribe she was cooking in that head of hers.

"This is my life."

"And this is my team. Hell, we don't even

know if we're at the right place." Luke looked at Holden for support. His friend of more than two years just shrugged.

So much for having his back.

Claire poked Luke's arm to get his attention. "Luke—"

"Easy. That's still sore."

"Steve is right. No one comes out here except the help. Look around you." She swept her hand out to the side, across the acres of crisp, green perfectly mowed grass and gentle hills. "It's the perfect place for Phil to hide."

"It's not exactly roughing it, either." Adam set his laptop down on the car and pointed at the photo of the front of the Samson manor home, then clicked through a series of other pictures. "This thing should be on a hill in Europe somewhere. There's an actual helicopter pad on the far end of the property. And what is that, like, ten thousand square feet under roof?"

To Luke it looked like five times that much. Beige stone reaching at least three stories high. There was an extra wing coming from the main house in a diagonal to the right and a row of garages to the left. He was surprised he didn't see a moat and a drawbridge.

If Phil was in there it could take a year and an entire police force to track him down. Luke knew he needed to shortcut that process.

"Have you tapped into the security feed?" Holden asked as he chugged the last of his coffee and squashed the cup in his fist.

"That's where this gets interesting." Adam clicked on a button and four images filled the screen. Four blocks, four big guys with even bigger guns.

"There a lot of crime out here?" Holden asked.

Claire made a clicking sound with her tongue. "He's in there. Leave it to Phil to live in greater luxury and with more security while in hiding than he did during his regular life."

Luke couldn't disagree because he knew she was right. Somewhere in that mass of firepower and maze of rooms sat Phil. Waiting, scheming, ready to pounce on Claire the minute he saw her.

Steve may not have figured it out, but Luke had. The minute the other man mentioned the house, a fissure of knowledge moved through Luke. Claire must have felt the same way, because she announced her discovery the second he'd walked into the safe house last night. They didn't talk about the other things Steve had said, only the house.

"I need to get in there and look around without getting my butt kicked or shot at. Again," he said.

Claire puffed out her chest. "I'll get you in."

Adam groaned as he turned away from the car.

Luke decided to make his dismissal of the idea even clearer. "That is never going to happen."

"I know the house plans. I know where Phil might be. You can't do this without me."

"Watch me."

"You said yourself the place is huge. I am the only hope we have to make it past the front door, with Adam's help on the alarms, of course."

"I thought you'd never been here before," Holden said.

About time his friend stood up and helped

out. "Exactly. You have as much information as we do. None." Luke said.

"Steve was wrong about that." She folded the map. "You don't think my attorney found this house? Look at it. Even my budget lawyer could look through records. This house was on the table at the time we started working on our divorce settlement agreement."

"Your attorney has some good contacts, then, because this was not easy to track," Adam said.

"My point is that Steve didn't know everything his brother was up to. If he did, that pension money might still be in its account."

"All good arguments, but no." Luke plucked the map out of her fingers. "It's too dangerous."

"I am the one Phil wants."

"That position does not work in favor of your argument." Luke slipped a microphone into his ear and glanced at Adam. "You're going to have to steer me through."

Adam shook his head. "I'll try."

"Since when is that good enough?"

"We have a disadvantage." Adam flipped the top of his laptop closed.

"You mean another disadvantage," Holden said.

"Yeah. See, the house plans on file with the county are interim plans and they don't match the house I'm looking at. That whole right side is new. I can't find anything about the construction and what's in there now. I can rig something through the camera feed, but I can't guide you from room to room."

"Which is why I am going in," she said.

Luke didn't think the pounding in his head could get any louder, but it did. "Absolutely not."

Holden laid a hand on Luke's shoulder. "Luke, she's going."

"Thank you." If she smiled any wider her eyes would disappear.

"It's not a compliment. I just know that unless I tie you to the steering wheel, you're going after him." Holden threw Luke a pitying look. "So just accept it and get moving."

Luke felt the ground shift beneath him. "You can't keep one woman in her place?"

Holden glanced at Claire and then back again. "Not this one."

"Then it's settled." She snapped the map out of his fingers before he could stop her. "Do I get a weapon?"

"I'm already regretting this," Holden said.

Luke frowned. "That makes two of us."

CLAIRE CROUCHED DOWN behind a hedge cut into the shape of a diamond. A four-foot diamond. Yeah, because having a big ol' house didn't make a strong enough expression of wealth. The Samson family went one step further and cut the rows of greenery that divided the garden from the pool in the shape of symbols from a deck of cards.

She wondered how she survived almost two years with Phil. And how she lived through the same time without Luke.

He ducked down beside her. He scanned the area, his eyes constantly taking in the surroundings.

"What's that building?" He pointed to one of the many structures sitting in the back half of the property.

She had no idea what it was. She had never been here. Didn't even remember Phil mentioning the place. Kind of hard to believe he just forgot he owned a multimillion-dollar property in the middle of horse country.

"The pool house." Because of its location, she engaged in some deductive reasoning. But really, the answer didn't matter. Phil wasn't hanging around outside. He lurked somewhere behind the heavy draperies.

"Where do you think he is?"

"Phil?"

"Who else would I be talking about?"

She knew, but she was stalling, trying to come up with the most logical response. "I think he could be…"

Luke's face fell. "You have no idea, do you?"

"Of course I do. I was married to him." When Luke didn't move, she gave up. "Okay, no."

"All that stuff about your attorney?"

"That wasn't true. I only said all of that so that you'd stop arguing about me coming with you. But how exactly could my attorney miss a house like this when he went searching for Phil's assets?"

"The part about you knowing the house?"

"A complete lie."

"Steve was right. You didn't know it existed."

"Didn't have a clue."

Luke sighed heavily enough to part her hair. "What's with all the subterfuge?"

"You were going to leave me behind."

"I still might."

"It's too late."

"Is that why you're telling me the truth now? You think I can't have Holden come in here and get you?"

"I'm saying it because it matters now. It was irrelevant then."

Luke smacked his lips together. "That pretty much sums up our entire relationship, doesn't it? You make whatever decision is best for you and screw me."

The abrupt turn in topic sent her stomach in free fall. "This probably isn't the right time for a 'what happened to us' discussion."

"I'm starting to think there's never going to be a right time."

"Then why did you bring it up?"

"I regret that I did." His gaze went to the speakers mounted around the outside area. "We know there are cameras out here somewhere because the Samsons love that sort of thing and the house plans we do have show a significant security operation downstairs. I'd bet they're hidden in those mountings."

As he droned on about wiring, something sharp and painful broke loose inside of her. The dam holding back all of the frustration and loss burst.

"You want to know why I left you?" The question was rhetorical because she sure as hell intended to tell him.

His eyes shifted to the side. "Uh, Claire…"

"I grew up with a man who hid the truth. He avoided questions and pushed my needs aside to focus on his own. When I woke up one morning and realized I was about to marry a man just like him—that's you—I panicked."

Luke's mouth dropped open. "Wait a second. You're comparing me to a con man?" Luke muttered under his breath.

She had suspected Luke wouldn't let that tidbit Steve delivered about her past slide by. She hadn't shared all that much with him about her parents. When Luke refused to open up, she returned the sentiment, closed off her emotions and prepared to leave. It took her longer than expected because despite it all, she loved him so much, but she knew she could not stay with a man just like her father.

"I didn't know, Luke. That's the point. You took a new job and started skulking around. You were out half the night."

He tapped on his ear. "We'll talk about this later."

"No, now. See, I didn't need to know every single detail about your past, but your present mattered."

"You were my present."

She refused to let that heartbreaking comment push her off task. "Do you know I followed you once? I was so sure you were cheating on me. I could close my eyes and smell perfume on your shirt."

"That's not true. I would never do that to you. To any woman. That is not who I am and you should have at least trusted me with that much." His harsh whisper carried the force of a punch.

"Don't you get it? I had no idea what you were capable of." When she realized how much her voice had risen, she swallowed and started again. "I didn't know you. You wouldn't let me in."

"Like how you didn't tell me about your dad?"

"I wanted to open up and tell you everything. I tried, but you kept cutting me off. You were always running out the door for your new job, the fake one." She snorted. "I always knew the antiques thing was a front. But when I asked you about it, about your life before me, you brushed me off."

Luke's fingers clenched around the tree branches. "So you ran off and married the first rich guy you met. Or maybe we overlapped."

"That is not true."

"The timing was awfully close."

"Because I saw what I thought was a sure thing and grabbed it. I found someone safe and stable who didn't remind me of all of the insecurities that came with living with a man I didn't know."

Luke's jaw hardened. "Okay, let's calm down."

"I had been through enough secrets and lies with my father. Watched him walk out never knowing when or if he'd come back. Then it all repeated with you." The words poured out of her. She wanted to pull back, but they kept coming. "I didn't like everything about Phil, but I knew who he was."

Luke sputtered. "Clearly not."

The bubble of emotion inside her popped. "Yeah. That's where I screwed up. My radar misfired. I ended up with the exact man I was trying to avoid."

"Is that my fault, too?"

She wanted to say yes. A few months ago she would have. Now the blame exhausted her, sucked the energy right out of her soul. "No."

A sudden calm washed over Luke. His features changed from sharp to flat. "You still think I'm a risk?"

She didn't. Not anymore. Not after watching him on the job, seeing him in protector mode. She knew the truth. He thrived on secrets but not the type that would destroy her. He was a good man, driven and sure. Leaving him had been the biggest mistake of her life. One she would pay for every lonely day until she died, which, if people kept shooting her, could be today.

"I think you're careful and guarded," she said.

"I don't know what that means."

"Ah, kids?" Holden's voice boomed in her right ear.

Claire's heart actually stuttered to a stop. "Oh, no."

Luke nodded. "Yeah."

She had forgotten all about the microphone and their audience back in the car at the end of the half-mile-long lane. Heat flashed over her entire body. If it was possible to blush from head to toe, she just did.

She glanced at Luke. When he threw her a half smile, she seriously considered throwing him in the bushes. "You could have warned me."

"In my defense, I tried," he said.

"When?"

"I pointed to the microphone in my ear."

"I thought you had an itch."

"This is interesting, really, but could we focus on clearing Claire of a murder that probably didn't happen before you two start throwing punches?" Holden didn't laugh, but she could tell by the lightness in his voice that he was fighting it off.

"Of course." She slugged Luke in his good shoulder. "Idiot."

"None of this would have happened if you hadn't married Phil," Luke shot back.

"I only did that because I was scared and you wouldn't tell me the truth."

Luke blew out a long breath. "Okay, look. I'm thinking Holden is right."

"Always," Holden said into the mic.

"Stop talking." She tried to clear her head of everything but the plan. Hunt down Phil and drag him into the precinct to clear her name. It sounded so simple. "Where next?"

Luke watched her for an extra second before getting back to work. "Adam?"

"I'm in the security system and can keep the screens on their end set to my picture long enough for you to slip in. Just let me know where and I'll set an infinite loop to give you the time you need."

"We want the easiest angle in." Luke's gaze went to a single door.

She followed his gaze. He managed to find the least impressive entrance. "Nothing fancy and no furniture in front of it."

"Probably means it leads to one of the least-used rooms, which is exactly what we need." Whatever Luke saw must have satisfied him because he brought the house blueprint up on his watch. "Adam, there's a door off a small patio on the far right."

A tapping sound filled the earphone. "It's a music room and it's clear."

Luke frowned at her. "Phil plays the piano?"

"I never saw it. Of course, I never saw this house, either, so what the heck do I know?" The fact that Phil hid all this from her didn't matter now, but it sure did tick her off. Nothing about Phil turned out to be real.

"How many exits once we're in?" Luke asked.

"Just two. Door to the patio and one to the hall."

"That will work." Luke scanned the open yard one last time. When he looked at her again a certain seriousness had washed over him. Gone was the confusion and arguing. "Stay down and follow me."

"You're in charge." She wasn't about to argue.

"About time you recognized that."

Chapter Ten

Luke smelled another setup. Getting around a wall of security, past the open space between the back patio and the house, and through a series of gates and locks should have been excruciating. He expected to dodge and hide, possibly fight off one or more of Samson's guards. Instead, they breezed through it all as if they'd been invited in the front door.

Alarms didn't blare. Cameras didn't shift to capture their movements. The back lock clicked open with very little pressure.

Too damn easy.

"What now?" Claire asked as she quietly shut the door behind her.

Luke stopped in the center and turned around in a full circle, hearing only the swoosh of his feet against the carpet. "Listen."

"I don't hear anything."

"Exactly. It's too quiet."

Except for the huge black piano sitting in the middle of the room, there wasn't much in there. A bunch of crystal bowls and figurines that only the rich would find interesting gleamed under a series of small lights. It all reeked of money, but none of it told a story about the people who lived there, except to say they spent money on useless junk.

"You think they left or we got it all wrong?"

"We weren't wrong."

"We seem to be alone in here."

The warning bell in his head tripped. "Where are the guards now, Adam?"

"Two out front by the entrance. That's about four miles from where you are right now, by the way."

"The other two?"

"One is on his way down the stairs. The other is in the kitchen. No one is near you. And from what I can tell, no one is manning the security station, either."

It all felt wrong.

"Holden? What do you think?" Luke asked.

"It's pretty relaxed at the moment. A good time to go in."

"I'm not so sure." Luke's voice didn't even rise to a whisper. He didn't want to raise the alarm prematurely.

"I went ahead and disabled the camera in your room just in case. You should be clear until you hit the hall. I can pick up again then. Just give me the signal," Adam said.

"I'm guessing we got lucky and the house is too big for them to hear one downstairs door open." Claire's voice filled with excitement as she spoke.

Luke didn't share her enthusiasm. He didn't believe in luck. Sometimes things worked out. Sometimes they were planned to happen. This smelled like the latter. "Maybe. Maybe not."

She stopped checking out the room and faced him. "What are you thinking?"

That they had walked right into the middle of a trap. Steve dropped a reference to this house, and Luke picked it up, thinking he'd found a piece of gold. He let the concerned-brother act fool him, even though it wasn't all that convincing.

"Talk about a con man."

"What?"

Luke pushed the coffee-shop memory from his mind. "Are you sure Phil never mentioned this place to you?"

She spread her arms. "I'd remember all this. Why?"

White-hot energy pumped through Luke. His body prepared for what his mind already sensed. "Something's very wrong."

Adam chuckled. "You always—"

His voice cut off.

Damn it. "Adam?"

Claire's eyebrows snapped together. "What's going on?"

The low buzz of static filled Luke's ear. "Adam. Check in."

"Why isn't he responding?" An edge of panic moved into her voice.

Luke let the anxiety spin until it fueled him. "Holden, you there?"

Nothing.

Claire tapped on her earpiece as if that would make the sound come out. "I can't hear them, either. What happened?"

Luke tried his cell but couldn't get a signal.

He peeked out the door to see if they had company. He knew that was inevitable now. "If I had to guess I'd say someone is jamming the signal. Trying to trap us in here without any eyes to the outside."

"That answers the question about whether we're alone."

"Exactly."

She gestured toward his wrist. "It's good we have your—"

Luke motioned for her to stop talking. He had downloaded the house's schematics, the only ones available, to his watch. Announcing that small advantage would steal any chance they might have to sneak up on someone.

He leaned down and whispered against her cheek, "Careful. Ears are everywhere."

Her gaze darted to the side. "Phil?"

Luke conducted a visual inspection of the room, looking for anything that might function as a secondary camera. Something Adam didn't know to scuttle. "That's why we're here. Chasing your not-so-dead ex all over the metro area."

"But how would he know we were coming?"

That was the simple part. "Because he was expecting us. He let us come right to him."

"I don't understand."

Luke could see the adrenaline pumping through her in the way her body trembled and her weight kept shifting from foot to foot. She didn't panic. Not his Claire. But she did look ready to bolt.

If Phil walked in right then, she might have choked him. Luke probably would have let her. The manipulative bastard of an ex-husband just kept crawling out and screwing her. Now he added Luke to his list of enemies. Luke viewed that as the other man's biggest mistake.

"This is part of the setup, Claire. Phil lured you—us—out here."

"Why?" Her mouth twisted in confusion.

The last drop of doubt in her story evaporated. Luke felt guilty that any still remained. "I'm not sure."

"That's not very comforting."

"What I mean is, I'm not sure what he has to gain here. It's all part of the plan."

Luke didn't have time to soothe or explain. Phil had been a very bad boy. This went deeper than hating his ex. The embezzlement and team of protectors suggested that Phil had a much bigger crime in mind. Probably hoped to skip out with the pension money and hang all that on Claire, as well.

Luke's gaze moved over the room looking for the one thing that didn't fit. A bulky statue on the piano grabbed his attention. The few pieces of art in the room were made of fragile crystal. All sat perfectly arranged under individual lights on the built-in bookshelves. The clay form of some unknown man was twice the size of anything else and totally out of place. Looked cheap, too.

"Phil knows exactly where we are." Luke wanted to hit something. Despite all the careful planning, Phil had stayed a step or two ahead.

She stared up at the ceiling. "He can see us?"

"Not if I can help it." Luke grabbed the statue and rubbed his thumb over it, checking for a seam or any evidence that it was something other than a priceless piece of art.

"You pick this moment to show an interest in antiques?"

"It's junk."

"No offense, but despite what you claim, you're not really an expert in that sort of thing."

"Don't have to be. I know a cover when I see one." He turned the item over and slid the bottom plate back. "Here it is."

The opening led to wires and a switch. And there, in the base, was a tiny window. A camera.

An image of every step they made traveled through the house and landed on a screen planted in front of Phil. When Luke found the guy, he planned to shove the camera down his throat. Let him choke on it. Until then, it was time to shut the information highway down.

He didn't need both arms for this. With a tight grip and a wide arc, he cracked the statue against the shelves. A sharp *thwack* sounded the second before the wood splintered, sending chips flying. The fake head rolled to the floor as the rest of the casing crumbled in Luke's hand.

"That's my kind of fine art," Luke said.

"Did you cut yourself?"

"No." He dropped the pieces to the floor and crunched them under his foot. "And so much for eavesdropping."

"I thought we were being quiet."

"Why bother? Phil already knows we're here. He's waiting. Watching. The object is to give him something he doesn't expect. Now that his mirror into this room is gone, we have that chance."

"How?"

"I don't know yet, but we need to get out of this room."

"Outside?"

"Too open. I don't know where Phil's men are. We could walk right into an ambush. And if I know Adam, he's doing double time trying to get the feed back up. Until he does, the key is to stay out of the camera range and get moving before the goons come sniffing."

"Claire."

Luke jumped at the sound of the deep voice bouncing off the walls. It echoed in the hall as if a loudspeaker blasted the message in every room.

"What the hell?" Luke asked the question of the room. He didn't expect an answer.

Claire had one. "That's Phil."

"He must be on some sort of intercom system. Guess that's one of those upgrades he made that's not on the plans anywhere."

"Does that mean he can still see us?"

"Since the sound's filling the whole house, I doubt it. If he knew we were still in here, we'd probably only hear it in here."

"Come into the entry and I will consider letting your boyfriend live," the faceless voice said.

Luke flashed Claire his harshest scowl. "If you move I'll…"

He trailed off when he realized he didn't have a believable threat ready.

She twisted her hands together hard enough to redden her skin. "Phil knows we're here. He has control over the guns and cameras. We don't have a choice."

"There's always another way. Besides, I'm armed."

"He could have Holden and Adam, for all we know."

Luke pushed that possibility out of his head. He could only handle one battle at a time and didn't need to invite more. "What are you suggesting?"

She pulled in tight to him, her feet planted between his, and held on to his forearms. Leaning in, she spoke in a voice so soft that only he could hear. "Let me."

This close he could smell the subtle hint of her shampoo and the fear that beat in her chest. "What?"

"I can go out there and talk to him."

The idea of that confrontation started a growl low in Luke's stomach. "The last time you tried to reason with this guy on his home turf you ended up as a murder suspect."

"He's not going to give up. Even if we do make it out of here, which I can't imagine, he'll hunt me down. He'll hunt you down."

"And we need to know why."

"Will it matter if we don't stop him? Luke, he's sent men to find us. He has men in the house to protect him now." The pleading in her dark eyes shouted louder than words.

"We've done fine so far." They had avoided and landed a few good shots. Even Luke wasn't sure how much longer that streak could last.

"Claire." Phil said her name in a singsongy voice. "It's time."

Her fingernails dug deeper into Luke's arms. He felt the pinch of pain but ignored it. She needed reassurance. If he could think of a way to fill her with hope, to pour it into her until the raw pain in her eyes disappeared, he would do it. But his mind went blank to anything but empty assurances. "We'll be okay. I promise."

"Don't you see? I can't let anything happen to you." Her tortured whisper battered his will.

"It won't."

"You don't know that."

"In case you haven't noticed, I can handle myself," he said, because he couldn't think of anything better to say.

She cupped his cheek in her palm as her eyes grew soft. "But I can't tolerate the idea of losing you."

The hard barrier around his heart eased up a fraction. "Claire—"

"I picked the wrong man last time. Let me do the right thing now."

Without touching her he could feel the determination radiating off her. There were so many things he wanted to say to her. He didn't even know what the right words were, but he wanted to stand there, staring into those eyes, as he fell for her all over again.

He settled for a harsh order. "There is no way you're going out there."

"Yes, I am. You are going to find Holden and Adam and get help. I'm going to stall for time. It's not a great plan, but it's the only plan."

Before he could protest she flattened both hands against his face and pulled him in closer for a world-shattering kiss. This time his hands slid up to her waist as the soft touch of her lips rocked him. His body shuddered from the impact as his eyes slipped closed.

His mind screamed to shut this down, but the rest of his body took charge. Heat flooded through him. In those precious moments, the seal, a promise, passed between them.

When her hands skimmed over his shoulders, he knew she was about to break off the kiss, stop the mad mix of danger and longing.

She jabbed her finger into his still-healing wound.

The shock of the violation sent a shout of fury rushing through him as his mouth broke from hers. Before he could push her away, she jammed her finger in harder, driving him to his knees and starting a fresh flow of blood down his arm.

When she finally let go, his body heaved in relief. But he couldn't stay on his feet. He crumpled to the floor, every nerve ending pulsing as his head spun. Random thoughts and slivers of pain assaulted his brain. He tried to ask her why, but the air refused to fill his lungs.

"I had to do it."

Doubled over, holding his throbbing arm, he struggled to clear his vision and shift back to his knees. His mind grabbed for any explanation for her behavior.

"Why?"

She placed a quick kiss on the top of his head. "It's my turn to save you."

The enormity of her actions pounded into him with the force of a car. She'd subdued him, nearly knocked him out with a blow of debilitating pain, so she could sacrifice herself.

He tried to reach out to her, but his arm wouldn't move. "Don't do this."

Worry and regret filled her gaze. "I'm sorry."

"Not this way."

"There's no other."

She blew him a kiss…and was gone.

Chapter Eleven

The walk from the music room to the main hall was the longest of Claire's life. Her legs dragged against the expensive marble floor as if each foot weighed more than the house. The screams of rage and fear in her head threatened to overwhelm her, but she kept moving. She had left her heart broken on the floor behind her. She needed her brain with her now, especially when she was doing something so unbelievably stupid and dangerous.

A bright light bathed the area in front of her. The tall windows drew in the sunshine, filling the round entry with a yellow glow. All that stood between her and the massive double doors to the freedom outside was a place in the dead center of the tile pattern on the floor. That and the determination to deliver Luke out of this mess in one piece.

"Claire." Phil's voice rang through the house once more.

"I'm coming, you crazy son-of-a—" When the uneasy sense of being stared at pricked at her, she stopped. Standing at the edge of the table, she pivoted and looked up at the staircase winding to the second floor behind her.

Stared right into the cold eyes of a dead man. One that was very much alive. Unfortunately. Tanned and fit with the same welcoming smile that fooled everyone, including her, for years. He had the nerve to wear the casual polo shirt she'd bought for his last birthday.

His gaze traveled over her. "I expected you yesterday."

"I had hoped you were dead."

He tsk-tsked her. "Is that any way to talk to your husband?"

"Ex."

"You forced me into that. I was satisfied to keep living separate lives."

"You mean sleeping around."

"I was discreet."

She suspected that last part. Never had the proof, but now she knew. On top of everything else Phil cheated on her. Couldn't even keep his zipper up for their short marriage. There was just nothing sacred to this man. What he showed on the outside clashed so sharply with the lack of substance beneath.

"You were pathetic. Still are," she said, meaning every word.

"If you had stayed I would have let you follow your dream of being an artist. Isn't that what you really wanted to do, instead of working as a property manager? Turn your little drawings into something profitable?"

"Let me?" She was appalled that she ever gave this man control over her life. Disgusted with him and furious with herself.

Phil shrugged. "I was willing to indulge you."

"Lucky me."

"Let you be whatever it was you wanted to be before we got married, and you stopped trying to be anything important."

The harsh words rang true, but she shook them off. Had to. If her mind wandered to the place where she relived every missed opportunity, she would be lost. Worse, she would lose Luke.

Phil wrapped his hands around the railing. "In return, all you had to do was understand that I needed to run my life as I pleased."

"When you put it that way, I wonder why I left. That's sarcasm, in case you couldn't tell."

Phil cocked his head to the side and shot her a look of false sympathy. "We both know the reason you insisted on the divorce."

"Which was?"

"The man who brought you here." Phil looked around and then opened his arms. "Where is your boyfriend? Your Mr. Hathaway."

"Luke is gone."

"You expect me to believe he'd walk away from you after all the trouble he went to over the past few days to keep you alive?" Phil barked out a harsh laugh. "I don't think so."

"I forced him."

"I doubt that. In fact, you seem to have charmed him. That's really the only explanation for why he would risk everything to sleep with a felon."

"I haven't been charged with anything." Not that she could be since the man was alive. But the idea of killing him now sure appealed to her.

"You are free because I allow you to be so."

"You own the police now?"

"You never appreciated the extent of my power."

"And you never realized the limits of your appeal."

"You cannot win here. You actually made my plan easier when you ran." Phil leaned against the railing. "I have to say, I didn't expect that. You always seemed so...practical."

"I guess that shows that you never really knew me at all."

"I could say the same of you."

No kidding. "What do you want from me?"

"You're going to come up here and we're going to have a little talk."

"I'm not moving."

"Oh, you will. I assure you."

She'd once found his self-assurance a sign of strength. Now she heard only the blowhard meanderings of a crazy person.

"I figure seeing you dragged up the stairs should bring your boyfriend out of hiding," Phil said, his voice low and menacing.

"I told you. He's gone." Part of her wanted Luke to flee to somewhere safe. Anywhere but this house on this day.

"We'll see." Phil glanced over her head and nodded.

Before she could duck or run, strong hands latched on to her upper arms. Instinct kicked in. She threw an elbow into the monster on her right as she tried to shift away from the one on her left. With feet moving, she struggled and thrashed.

The blow came out of nowhere. A sharp knock to the back of her head that caused her legs to collapse under her. Balance deserted her as gravity pressed her down. The men didn't try to hold her. The force of her knees hitting the floor cut off her breath. An agonizing burn radiated through the lower half of her body. She clamped down on the yelp, cutting it off before it could fully form into the traumatized scream rattling around inside her.

She didn't want Luke to come running or for Phil to enjoy her weakness. A few deep breaths helped her to wrestle back her control. When she finally worked up the strength to move her neck again, she saw the confident smile on Phil's face.

He motioned to his men. "Bring her up here."

THEY WERE GOING to kill her.

That thought ran through Luke's mind as he grabbed for the doorknob and pushed to his feet. While the blurring at the edge of his vision started to clear, the throbbing in his arm only increased.

To stem the bleeding he ripped the bottom of his shirt and tied the cloth around the juncture of his arm and shoulder. The tight band didn't do anything to stop the thumping, but at least he could move again without leaving a blood trail behind him.

He managed two steps before he heard Claire's strangled cry. The sound knocked the last of the dizziness out of his system.

With his gun in his hand, he whipped around the corner, forcing his heartbeat to slow and his mind to concentrate. Running in at the wrong time could get Claire killed. He had to be smarter. Be patient.

He hit the entry just in time to see two goons pull Claire up the steps behind them. Luke flattened against the wall before they could notice him. But he saw her. The limp. The grimace when she put weight on her left leg. They'd hurt her. In the few minutes it took for his mind to clear, they'd hurt her.

It would take him even less to carry out his revenge for her pain. One bullet should do it.

When the bulky male figures disappeared out of sight and the beat of footsteps stopped, Luke took off. He crept across the entry to the front door. Looking up behind him, he saw nothing but an empty balcony. Luke vowed to find her. First he looked out front. No goons. The two with Claire were probably the two that Adam reported being together. That left two more unaccounted for.

With slow, sure steps he slipped to the bottom of the stairs. He eased his weight up one stair at a time, careful to keep his weight balanced and the chance of creaking to a minimum. With his injury acting up all over again, he leaned his sore side against the staircase railing as he went.

When he got to the top he prayed the action would be to his left. He had the floor plans, or a version of them, for all the rooms on the left. The right was new and a mystery. Getting around there without any intel or assistance from Adam could prove impossible.

Even now Luke hoped that whatever Adam had done to knock out the security cameras continued to work. Since no one showed up to shoot him or push him down the stairs, he held on to that hope.

The low grumble of voices grew louder the higher he climbed. With all the stone and hard surfaces, sound bounced around the cavernous place, hiding its true origin. He stopped, trying to get his bearings and pick out Claire's husky voice. But he couldn't make out the words, could barely tell who spoke.

The hard floor was carpeted on the second floor. The plush pile muffled the sound of his footsteps as he turned first to the right, then the left. From here he could tell that Phil held her on the right.

Advantage, Phil.

The man had planned for this, possibly from the first minute he met Claire. Maybe he recognized the vulnerability under all that sexy strength. It was one of the things that attracted Luke.

Not that he would admit to having anything in common with Phil. Luke refused to believe that. Where he loved Claire, Phil used her. Phil might have said the right things at the right time, but Luke meant them. He just hoped like hell that he had the opportunity to make her believe them this time.

He passed the first two doors, checking his watch for any indication of what was ahead. The internal GPS put him off the grid.

He was on his own.

Chapter Twelve

Claire sat in a chair with two thugs looming over her from behind and one guy staring at her head-on. She knew from a quick visual inventory that she was in some sort of library. Dark shelves filled with books she'd bet Phil never read. A huge mahogany desk and an even bigger red leather chair filled with Phil and his smug smile.

"So," he said, and then let the word just sit there.

No way was she engaging. She was too busy making a mental note of the exits and setting the furniture in the floor plan she'd created in her head.

Phil twisted a pen between his fingers. "Don't you want to know why you're here?"

When she didn't answer, Phil nodded to

one of the men behind her. She braced for the shot she knew would come. Just as she inhaled, the man landed a repeat smack to the back of her head. The sudden shock of pain brought tears to her eyes. She grabbed the armrests, digging her nails deep into the soft leather, to keep from crying out.

Phil laughed. "Nicely done."

Her attacker grunted in response.

"Are you ready to talk now?" Phil asked.

Since she didn't know how many hits she could take before she gave in to a concussion or worse, she relented. "What do you want, Phil?"

"You."

The thought of letting him touch her again brought a rank taste to her mouth. "Never."

"Don't flatter yourself. You were good, attractive, but utterly forgettable."

He probably thought the comment meant something. That it would break her, but it just showed how little he knew. The insult struck her as a feeble attempt by a pathetic and desperate man.

"If I'm so unimportant, then why the big need to track me down? These morons are only the latest you've sent after me." She hitched her thumb at the men behind her. "You've got to be running low on henchmen willing to do your bidding."

"When you ran I had to improvise." Phil tapped one end of the pen against the desk blotter before returning to the frenzied flipping in his hand. "It gave me time to refine your role in my murder and the company's yet-to-be-discovered embezzlement."

"I can't believe you actually stole from the people who work for you."

"The money belongs to me."

"Are you insane?"

He flashed her a smile that hinted at malice more than madeness. "I assure you, no."

"It's their retirement security, not yours. You didn't earn any of it. They put their money in accounts for years. They trusted you to invest it and expected—"

He slammed the pen against the desk. "Spare me the lecture. It sounds hollow coming from a woman who climbed into my bed to get her hands on my checkbook."

She looked into his eyes and knew he

believed it. That's how he saw her. Only, his opinion didn't matter.

"That is not true, Phil. It was never about getting my hands on your money."

"It wasn't a secret. I knew. My family knew. The people at the club saw through the outer shell of confidence you presented. Sure, you tried to adapt, but underneath you never stopped being the throwaway kid of a bigamist."

She should have guessed he had checked into her background, even though he'd never asked her or seemed to care. After being stung by Luke, she had welcomed the idea of not getting in too deep, of just living in the moment without a huge investment of emotion. Loving without limits had cost her everything. She'd learned that lesson the hard way.

But while she created a distance from Phil, it looked as if he had his own plan. If she guessed right, the entire marriage had been a setup for this moment. That meant finding a victim. She'd unwittingly played the role so well.

"Why did you marry me?" she asked, wanting to know for the first time.

"I thought you might prove useful."

The words slapped against her already bruised skin. She didn't care what he thought, because he'd ceased to be important soon after they walked down the aisle. But the idea that she sold her dreams and crushed her hopes of being with Luke because she was afraid, because her father's actions taught her not to trust or believe in love, made her stomach heave. She ran from her father's image and a man who was good for her to Phil, a man who wanted to destroy her.

Here she'd thought she'd spent her life fighting for control when, really, she let the men she knew determine the roads she traveled. The reality of her missteps pummeled her.

"That's funny because I thought the same thing about the Samson name. Might be useful, but I was wrong."

"If you were really looking for love and forever, why didn't you marry your salesman?"

"My what?"

"Isn't that what Luke does? He trades and sells antiques." Phil's face crumpled in mock shame. "Really, Claire. Did you think he could give you the money and prestige you so desperately craved?"

Claire almost laughed at how far from the truth that assessment of Luke proved to be. "You never said why I'm here."

"I need you to sign some papers."

The hit to the head must have scrambled something. She couldn't think of another explanation for what she thought she'd heard. *"What?"*

"The evidence against you is strong. I should know because I planted most of it, but since I don't want any do-gooder cop who's looking to make a name for himself seeing those big sad eyes of yours and deciding to dig deeper, it would help if your fingerprints were actually on the incriminating documents. Fingerprints and signatures. The e-mails have been planted. This is just something extra."

"You're crazy."

"I'm leaving town with twenty-eight million dollars in my offshore accounts and a pile of debt behind me. I can guarantee you that is the sign of being smart, not crazy."

"I'm not going to help you."

"Yes, you are."

A hand clamped down on the back of her neck and pushed her head forward. The position crushed her windpipe and had her gasping. With each breath the knocking at the back of her skull increased.

When the pressure eased, her head flew up but her brain kept rattling. "Phil—"

"These men are prepared to make the next hour of your life very unpleasant. Your choice is simple. You can do what I tell you, and in return, you'll die quickly." Phil smiled. "As will your boyfriend. Or we can make it last."

Her throat grew thick and closed at the idea of anything happening to Luke. "I told you he's gone."

"I'll bet he's just a few steps away, waiting to jump in here and play the role of rescuer."

She hoped Phil was as wrong about that as he was about everything else. "What if he does?"

"He'll die fast, but you'll get the slow torture option."

Her mind raced with questions, ways to stall for time. Jumping out the window in a mangled heap would ruin Phil's plans but not bring her one step closer to saving Luke.

And where was he? She knew she'd inflicted damage. Saw it in the raw pain that flashed in his eyes as she put on the pressure and threw him to the floor.

But she knew Luke. Recognized the bone-deep stubborn streak that would keep him from giving up. Somehow he would find her.

"How are you going to pin all these crimes on me if I'm dead?" she asked.

"That part is taken care of." Phil tipped his head to the side. "So what will it be?"

"As far as I'm concerned I've done enough for you."

"Then torture it is." Phil's smile widened. "Perfect."

Chapter Thirteen

Luke wiped the sweat off his forehead with his arm as he stood on the balcony with his back pressed against the brick wall of the house. From two rooms down he could hear pieces of the conversation, mostly Phil's end, since he delivered every word as if he was standing on a stage. But Luke got the gist. Claire's time had just run out.

He slipped back into the bedroom. Picked up the phone on the nightstand, hoping this one would work where the two others he'd found in the house didn't. He had tried to dial and only got silence in return. They were as useless as the cell in his pocket. Phil had some sort of jamming device set up on the property. Luke recognized the technology. He was just surprised Phil had thought that far ahead.

Despite the numbness in his shoulder and the questions spinning in his head, Luke knew he had to move. He would only get one chance to surprise the two gun handlers in the room. Take them out and get Claire to the floor. Then he could go after Phil. No matter how many bullets pumped into him, he knew he could stay on his feet long enough to take Phil out.

Luke stepped closer to the open doorway. Heard the whack of a hand against a face, Claire's face, and checked his gun.

After a silent count of three, he flipped around the corner. "Claire, get down!"

With gun raised and firing, he hit Phil's men in the backs of their legs. Each dropped to the floor screaming like the wounded animals they were as he pumped additional rounds into them.

When the constant banging ended, Luke stood over Claire's curled form. He reached down to scoop her off the floor. Before he could touch her, she jumped off the carpet and slammed against his chest.

"You came." She repeated the mantra over and over again.

"You're okay," he said as he brushed his hand up and down her arm, as if searching for injuries.

Luke noticed Phil hadn't moved. But she was alive. For a few wrenching moments he feared she had gotten caught in the cross fire. Then he realized that neither of the other men had gotten off a shot. Even now, one lay still and the other squirmed and moaned, but the end would overtake him soon.

The jump of surprise had worked.

Luke used his foot to drag their weapons close. He tried to wrap his arm around Claire, but he had no strength left in his ripped-up shoulder. He settled for bringing her in close to his side, tucking her head against his throat, while he trained his weapon on Phil.

The anxious jumping in Luke's chest slowed for the first time since he'd seen Claire across that lobby days ago. He smiled at Phil. "Surprise."

Luke strained to understand the mumbled words of apology Claire pressed against his neck, but he couldn't truly enjoy the moment. Not with Phil just sitting there. The man hadn't so much as shifted in his chair. He sat with hands folded in front of him and watched the horror scene unfold. He didn't rush for a weapon or the door, didn't even shout a warning to his men before Luke's fury was unleashed.

Phil finally tipped his head. "Very impressive for a salesman."

Claire squeezed Luke's waist with her arm. She continued to shake. "He thinks you peddle art."

"I don't care what he thinks." Luke nodded to the phone next to Phil's hand. "Pick it up."

"I would, but the line appears to be dead."

So calm. Phil didn't act like a man whose world had just collapsed. His breathing remained even and his movements fluid.

Made Luke think the other two of his men were close by. "Get up."

"I am fine where I am," Phil said.

"Just shoot him," Claire said, her voice gaining in strength as she found her footing again. She stood up straight and stared at Phil with a look that promised pain and retribution.

In that moment Luke wanted the other

man dead. Punished and destroyed. The temptation to put a bullet in Phil's head pulled at Luke. He had spent his professional life following the law. This one time, he wanted to break it. He had never craved another man's agony the way he craved for Phil's.

"I said, stand up," Luke said before he could fire that gun and fundamentally change who he was as a human being.

"Let's just grab him and get out of here." Claire made her plea from right behind him.

"I intend to." Luke took two more steps and stopped right in front of the desk.

Suddenly he heard footsteps behind him. He didn't sense the trap until it sprang. He turned around in time to see Steve pointing a gun at the back of Claire's head.

"Were you expecting me?" Steve asked as he kicked at the men littering the floor.

Claire jumped at the sound of her former brother-in-law's voice. She tried to move away, but Steve had her arm and the gun dug into her skin.

Luke bit back the string of profanity sitting on his tongue. He blinked and they swooped.

For a second he let his desire for vengeance overtake his common sense. And Claire was going to pay the price.

Phil finally stood up. “Lower your gun or she dies.”

Claire’s eyes grew wide. “Luke, don’t do it.”

Luke shifted his gaze between the other men. Steve’s hatred for Claire radiated off him in waves. He wanted her gone and he had the will to do it. The dangerous combination made rushing him a poor solution.

“Do it now, Mr. Hathaway,” Steve said.

“Do not test me. Just hand it over.” Phil extended his palm.

Luke knew the cardinal rule: never surrender your weapon. But the battle between heart and head was an easy one, thanks to the gun aimed at Claire.

Luke turned his gun around and handed it to Phil. “Here.”

Claire gasped and reached out. “Luke, no!” She stopped when Steve shook her. The hard action made her head bounce as if barely attached to her body.

Luke took a step in her direction. “Let her go.”

"You are not in charge here."

When Steve pressed the gun harder against her skull, Luke had to block the image from his mind. If he saw the dizzying pain in her eyes or heard her moan again, he would lose it. Snap so hard he'd never return to normal.

Instead, he decided to test the brotherhood bond. "So, which one of you is in charge?"

"Me." Steve motioned toward the desk and shoved Claire in its general direction. "Sign."

When her eyes met his, Luke nodded. She walked across the carpet with careful steps, putting more weight on her left than her right. She grabbed the pen Phil offered and signed where he pointed.

"This is never going to work, you know," Luke said, concentrating his attention on Phil, whom he considered the weaker of the two.

Steve answered. "Shut up."

"You have a lot of bodies piling up. You think people are going to believe Claire accomplished all that while the cops were on her tail?"

"That's why it was so convenient for her to run. Took away what otherwise would have been her security. Made it easy for us to continue to set her up."

The pages flipped as Claire signed whatever it was the Samson brothers found so important. "And when the police eventually find us?" she asked.

"We will be far away from here. Even if the police track the money and ignore the trail we planted to Claire's door, it won't matter. We will have everything we need."

"All this for money?" Luke asked, knowing the answer was yes.

She shrugged. "When a house falls, it falls."

"What does that mean?"

"The money is long gone," Steve said.

The pieces finally fit. The Samson family wealth was illusory. "You built your empire on the dollars of investors, but the underlying capital had been spent. Now that the cash flow has stopped, you don't have any money left to pay back the people you owe."

Phil folded his arms across his stomach. "You're quick for a salesman."

The enormity of the situation hit Luke. This was all about something as simple as stealing. People dead and Claire ruined all over money. "This is about a pyramid scheme? You guys committed fraud and don't want to serve any time."

"Do you blame us?" Phil asked.

Luke decided right then that he would never understand the thinking processes of rich people with overdeveloped senses of entitlement. "Why not sell this house or one of the twenty other houses you own?"

"We've taken out all the equity we can without tipping off the authorities. Well, according to the paperwork Claire is signing, she's the one who did it."

When she stopped, Phil shoved her to get her moving again.

"Claire will be held responsible, but we'll take the money with us." Steve brushed aside the curtain and stared out into the backyard. "It is up to the banks to figure out the rest. It will probably take years to sort through it all."

"You're just thieves." Luke could think of other names to call them, but settled on that one.

"You have yourself to blame. After all, you provided me with the perfect ending.

All I had to do was mention this house and here you came." Steve shared a hearty laugh with his brother. "It was so easy. I could see the gears grind in your brain as you sat there pretending to drink your coffee."

"Why don't I show you something else I can do?" Luke asked.

"Stay where you are." Steve glanced at Claire, then Phil. "Is she done?"

Phil leaned down to scan the pages. Luke watched as Claire slid the pen down to her palm, grasping it like a weapon.

Good woman.

They had seconds only, but somehow she had figured out a way to squeeze them out of the dire situation. He balanced, ready to jump on Steve. The man looked comfortable with a gun, but that didn't mean he ever left the safety of his desk to shoot one. If his shot went wild, they stood a chance.

Claire looked around the room one more time before lifting her arm. With a *whoosh,* her hand slammed down on top of Phil's. The point of the pen entered the back of his hand. Phil's hysterical screams followed right after.

"What did you do?" Steve roared.

But Luke was already moving. He crashed into Steve using his injured side. There was no time for anything else. As Phil stalked around behind his desk, Luke fell on top of Steve. Their bodies hit the carpet before Luke could brace for the fall.

Despite his superior physical condition, the mix of the injury and awkward position gave Steve the extra second to step back and only endure a fraction of the knock heading his way. In a smart move Luke didn't know Steve had in him, he shook off his daze from the fall and kept moving.

Like everyone else, he went right for the bandage. A beefy hand clamped down on the blood-soaked area. Through gritted teeth, Luke struggled, only stopping when Phil yelled his name. The high-pitched snarl matched the rage in his eyes. Phil held Claire around the neck with the tip of the pen aimed directly at the artery pumping there.

Luke froze. "Don't hurt her."

"I am going to kill her and make you watch."

"It's okay." She repeated the words several times until Luke didn't know if she was convincing him or her.

"Phil, not yet. Putting a bullet in her now will ruin our plans." Due to the extra weight around his middle, Steve grabbed on to the chair to get off the floor. But he never relaxed his hold on the gun. If he had, Luke would have been all over him.

Luke sat on the floor with the dull roar of pain vibrating through every part of his body. He doubted he would ever feel the sweet freedom of a normal moment again.

But he got what he wanted. One of the guard's guns was tucked under his thigh. Hiding it would be the problem. Without a jacket and with Claire still in the direct line of fire, he had to be careful.

Steve pointed the gun at Luke's head. "You have five seconds to get up."

He palmed the weapon, rolling it under his shoe as he made a show of struggling to his feet.

"Luke, please…" Claire's voice trailed off as his head rose above the edge of the desk and into her line of vision. When her face turned milk white, he knew he looked bad.

But inside the fight remained. The left half of his upper body had turned soft and useless, but he had Claire on his side. Together they could get through this. Somehow.

"It's time to go." Steve frowned at Phil. "And clean up that mess."

Phil turned his hand and saw the blood dribbling to his wrist. His reaction was immediate. He tightened his hold on Claire's neck until she gagged and gasped for air.

"Stop!" Luke yelled the command.

When he made a move to follow it up with action, the barrel of Steve's gun pressed into his temple. "No one moves unless I say so," Steve said.

The more she fought and the harsher the guttural scratching in her throat became, the wider Phil smiled.

Steve finally ended his brother's show of unnecessary macho strength. "We have plans for her that do not include bleeding out in the library."

After one more tug, Phil let go. Claire's hand fell to the desk for balance as ragged coughs shook her body. After a decp inhale, she stood up.

Her gaze went right to Luke's. "I'm fine."

Phil laughed. "For now."

Chapter Fourteen

Phil used a tissue to grab the papers Claire had just signed. Touching the edges, he threw them into a briefcase, then marched her around the desk. As they met up with Luke on the other side, he grimaced.

She didn't think she had an ounce of emotion left in her, that it had all been drained away, leaving behind only aches and cuts. But seeing such a strong man brought down sent a new wave of sadness washing through her.

She rushed to Luke's side. "What is it?"

He grabbed his shoulder and bent over, moaning. Before she could comfort him, Phil delivered a blow to Luke's back. Luke fell to the carpet, sprawling on his stomach, and went still.

"Luke!" Seeing him crumple like that shredded what was left of her sanity. She bent down to help him back up.

He could not die like this.

Phil poked Luke's side with his shoe. "Get up, Hathaway."

"Stop it!" She threw out her hands and tried to put her body between them. "He's hurt."

Steve grabbed her by the elbow and lifted her to her feet. "He's going to be a dead puddle on the floor if he doesn't start moving."

Luke held up a hand. "I'm fine. I can do it."

He rose first to his knees and then the whole way up. When he cradled his shoulder across his stomach and blood oozed through his fingers, she knew he had taken too many blows. The constant pounding and loss of blood had made him woozy. She could see it in his staggering steps. His mouth stretched into a grim line as he tried not to wince.

She brushed her palm over his back as she swallowed a sob of regret. "Are you okay?"

"There will be plenty of time for the two of you to say goodbye later." Phil smiled at the comment, clearly proud he'd come up with it.

Claire ignored the Samson brothers. She had wiped them out of her life and now she would clear them from her mind. Her only concern was Luke. She stole a few sideways glances at him as Phil ushered them down a long hall with a gun at their backs.

She regretted every decision of the past week. Heck, of the past two years. She should have stayed and fought for Luke, for them. Having blown up everything good around her, she should have run and kept on running. Not involved Luke in her mess of a life. She had forced him to do this, to risk his life for her, by following his steps and reappearing in front of him long after he had moved on.

And now he would die. The crushing pain of that realization slowed her steps.

"I think you'll like the work we've done here," Phil said. "Added a few rooms, including a special one we've fixed up just for you two."

She blocked out the words and concentrated on sending Luke a silent message. She loved him. In the shadow of what once was, she had grown to love him even more. Gone was the fantasy of a perfect, quiet life. She now understood that Luke had offered her more—a lifetime of commitment and fidelity, love and protection. She had pushed it, and him, away.

Maybe he could no longer say the words or give her every piece of information she needed, but that didn't matter. She would cherish every precious moment she'd ever had with him. Hold them close until the very end.

"Stop." Steve positioned them in front of a locked door. He flicked open the keypad next to the door and punched in a code.

Only these two brothers would have private rooms in their huge private mansion. She tried to see over Steve's shoulder what required so much secrecy.

Phil pulled her back. "That's close enough."

When the wall monitor beeped, Steve shoved the door open and gestured for them to walk inside. Not knowing what lingered over the threshold, she hesitated. But there was nothing all that special about this place except for what was missing. No windows. No chairs. Just a desk in the middle of the room, a safe and walls painted dark brown. It was the most depressing decor she'd ever seen, and it did not match the overstyled look of the rest of the house.

She glanced at Luke to see his reaction. He stayed huddled over his arm, as if he had lost touch with the horrors of their situation and slipped into a world only he understood. In a way she figured that might be a good thing, because she continued to live right here in reality, dreading every second.

"What is this place?" she asked as she maneuvered Luke to the table and let him lean against it. He needed to preserve what little energy he had left.

Steve stood right behind her, his breath right on top of her. "It was going to be a panic room of sorts. We didn't get a chance to finish it, but it will do for our purposes."

"Now it will be the place where you die." Phil leaned on the door looking satisfied with his plan.

She waited for the shots to come. Instead, the brothers stood there, staring at her.

"Don't you want to know how?" Phil asked.

"I'm sure I'll figure it out in a few seconds."

Steve tapped on the small computer screen just inside the door. "From here you can watch us walk down the hall. We're going to leave."

Phil nodded. "And you're going to stay."

She figured she missed the part where they shot her. "And?"

"We want the authorities to find your bodies intact. Otherwise, your boyfriend would be dead." Phil frowned. "Not that he's all that alive anymore, anyway."

She shifted her weight onto her sore leg. The throbbing started immediately, but she didn't move. She wanted to block any shot Phil might take at Luke.

"The police will find the evidence they need to figure out you died while planning your escape, and we'll be far away. Safe," Steve added.

Phil's smile turned feral. "With all the money."

They could not be dumb enough to leave her alive. She knew there had to be something else. Despite that, hope flickered inside her. If she could rouse Luke, they might be able to break down the door or crash through the wall.

As if he read her mind, Steve started shaking his head. "You will not be able to weasel out of here. It is not fully outfitted, but the room was built for security. And I assure you it is very secure."

"Unfortunately for you, it will function to keep you in, instead of keeping other people out," Phil said.

For guys who needed to leave, they sure were doing a lot of talking. But every second they stood there gave Luke another second to heal, so she didn't question it.

"Why would you even need a room like this?" she asked.

"You never know." Steve pointed his gun at the monitor again. "Just watch this and you'll see when you're about to die."

Phil took a step toward her. "Death will come racing down the hall in a few minutes. I want you to know it, breathe it in and be unable to escape it. Think of it as part of our divorce settlement."

"Not being married to you is gift enough."

"Now, don't be like that." Phil dropped his head to the side in that annoying way only he could do. "How about a farewell kiss?"

"If you come within a foot of me, I will bite you. And there's no telling where I'll aim."

Phil barked out a laugh. "If you had been that feisty during the marriage, I might have cut you in on the deal."

"I don't want anything to do with you."

Phil took another step. "So be it."

"Enough." Steve grabbed his brother by the arm and pulled him back. He nodded his head toward the door. "It's time."

After some silent message passed between them, both men backed out.

"Enjoy your final minutes with Mr. Hathaway," Steve said with a dramatic bow.

She heard their demented laughter as they shut the door, locking Luke and her tight inside. When she turned back to Luke, his head popped up and he smiled.

"Sounds like we need to move fast," he said in a clear voice. "Not sure what this racing-death thing is all about, but I don't really want to find out."

Her stomach dropped heavy and hollow to

her knees. "I thought you were so hurt that you couldn't move."

"All an act to get my hands on this." He held up a gun.

"Where did that come from?"

"One of the guards."

The confusion and fear bottled up inside her morphed into fury. "You mean you were fine the whole time?"

"I was pretending." His voice suggested she should just get over it. "I needed to buy time and grab a weapon. I figure those two would feel more manly and be less likely to attack again if they thought I was subdued. Also gave me time to get in position in the event I had to fire off a shot."

Luke made it sound so simple. She thought it was the exact opposite. "Well, genius, what if they had tried to shoot me?"

"Yeah, that's where I thought they were going."

She took one step, got close enough to smell his earthy scent, and then shoved with all her might against his uninjured shoulder. "You jerk!"

His chest absorbed her hit. "Hey!"

"What?"

He frowned at her and had the nerve to look offended. "What is wrong with you?"

"I thought you were…"

"Asleep?"

"Destroyed, Luke. I thought they'd broken you." The words tumbled out of her. "When you curled up on the floor, a piece of me dropped there with you. I didn't think you could function."

Instead of being reassured, he looked appalled. "Why would you think that?"

Clearly she had struck a blow against his manliness. While she was at it she decided to level one more verbal shot. "You all but wept like a baby in there."

"It's called acting."

"I could shoot you myself right now." She turned away from him because she didn't want to see his smug face. Not when tears pushed against her eyelids and her body trembled with relief.

"Claire." He wrapped his arm around her from behind. "I was ready to kill them both. I would have if they made one move in your direction."

She brushed her fingers over the back of his hand and settled into his warmth. Even through the red haze of her anger, being next to him filled her with comfort. In the middle of complete madness she experienced a second of calm.

But she wasn't ready to forgive. "Why didn't you use the gun and end this?"

"You were right in the middle. I refuse to risk your life even further. The chance of me getting two rounds off before they fired was not a sure thing." He kissed the side of her neck.

She tilted her head to the side to give him a better angle. "You had the advantage. You're in law enforcement. They're just two crooked businessmen."

"With a shooting range at the back of the property."

Her heart fell to her knees. "Oh, I missed that."

"I saw it when I was hanging off the balcony earlier. Either way, I still didn't like the odds."

"Why?" She glanced up at him and slumped in relief at seeing clear eyes gaze back at her.

"Because without the absolute guarantee that you'd be safe, I wasn't going there."

Her heart tripped and fell. Love. The nothing-else-matters kind. The sure sort of love that ignored small slights and reveled in being together. She loved him before, but this was so much more. She didn't need him to complete her. She needed him for life to make sense.

Right now she also needed him to get her out of there. "I don't mean to be negative, but we're stuck."

"Not really."

She broke out of his grasp and turned around to face him. "You plan to shoot our way out?"

"I plan to open this lock like I do every other lock." He held up his wrist and shook his watch at her.

"It can't be that easy."

"They should have smashed the monitor."

"They were pretty clear that there's something out there they want us to see."

Luke stalked over to the monitor and stared. "There's nothing out there." Then he started punching numbers.

"What are you doing?"

"Making sure it's not booby-trapped."

"Fabulous." She walked over to the safe and yanked on the door. It wouldn't budge. "Wonder what's in here."

"Probably whatever it is they think will implicate you."

"Then why have me sign all of those other papers?"

"Insurance." He slipped a small knife out of his waistband and started undoing the panel covering the keypad. "The idea was to leave a significant paper trail."

"How enterprising." She slouched down on top of the safe. "If Phil had put half this effort into his company, he wouldn't have had to steal from his employees."

"It doesn't work that way."

"Meaning?"

"The bad guys always go for the easy solution. Usually they can't handle the hard one."

She threw out her arms. "This was easy? They had this elaborate setup. They hired these men, so that means paying people. And this house is ridiculous."

Luke snorted. "Expendable."

"What?"

"Nothing." He set the panel on the floor. "They were buying time as they looted the funds."

For a guy she thought was near death just minutes ago, he sure did sound chipper. "What are you doing now?"

"Seeing if I can blow this thing."

"I thought you planned to use your watch."

"I don't know where the Samson boys are. If they're still downstairs, I don't want to tip them off. Not if I can just open this the usual way."

"Usual?"

"By figuring out the code." He poked around, then made a clicking sound with his tongue. "Forget it. We'll take the chance."

"Works for me. I just want out of here." Even with Phil and Steve gone, her stomach kept jumping with nerves. She couldn't settle the feeling of anxiety that moved through her and gained speed with every circle.

"Two seconds." He pulled a wire out of the side of his watch and connected it to the panel.

"We don't have that much time."

It was more like a minute, but his shoulders finally relaxed. "There."

The door clicked open.

Neither of them rushed into the hall. Heeding Steve's warning, they waited for something to rise up and attack. But nothing came.

Luke held up a finger. "Wait here."

"No." She slid off the safe and walked over to him. "We do this together."

"I don't know what's out there," he said in a whisper.

"I know what's in here and it's not freedom, so I'll take my chances so long as I'm going in the direction of an exit."

"Well said."

He leaned down and treated her to a quick, hard kiss. Just enough to get her wanting more.

She held on to his shirt, keeping him close for a few precious seconds. "Besides, I watched you collapse once. I will not wait around and then stumble over your body at the bottom of the stairs."

Something sparked to life in his green eyes. "Have some faith."

"In you? Completely."

He winked at her. "Then let's do this."

They got into the hall before she smelled it. She coughed when she tasted the acrid scent on her tongue. It was a mix of chemicals and hot metal.

Her gaze went to the soaring ceiling. Gray smoke hovered along the sloped walls. She was afraid to lean over the balcony to the floor below. “I think I know what Steve wanted us to see.”

Luke nodded. “They set the house on fire.”

Chapter Fifteen

Luke tried to figure out what else could go wrong. Short of killer bees, they'd survived everything. So far.

The flames licking up the banister could be the final shot. Bright orange filled the downstairs and began the slow walk up the stairs. There was no way through it. They'd have to go around it.

Claire covered her mouth with the back of her hand as a coughing fit overtook her. "I can't breathe."

And it was only going to get worse.

He covered his mouth with his shirt and grabbed her hand. The fire hadn't reached the landing where they stood. He debated crossing to the other wing, the one where he could call up a floor plan and pray for a set of back stairs. But once they were over there, they'd be trapped.

"Do you know if there's another way down?" she asked through her sleeve, which was now wadded up and covering her mouth.

He tried to call up the layout from memory. Nothing came to him. The only sure thing was the long balcony that extended from the bedrooms where he hid earlier.

"Must be, but I don't know where."

She buried her face in his arm. "What do we do?"

Whatever choice they made, they had to do it now. Thick gray smoked swelled, floating higher to surround them. Intense heat cut off the oxygen until every breath burned down his throat and into his lungs.

He grabbed her hand. "This way."

They crouched down, trying to find a pocket of clean air, but smoke covered everything now. The space grew thick and black. Every step dragged as his vision clouded.

He dragged his hand along the wall, counting doors as he went. He depended on his memory to guide him. At the fourth door, they ducked inside.

He slammed the door shut behind them and inhaled the cleaner air. "We should have a few minutes."

"Here." She stripped a blanket off the bed and handed it to him.

As he shoved it under the door, tucking in the corners to block as much of the seam as possible, he gestured to her to open the entrance to the balcony. "We need fresh air."

Since she continued to wheeze, he knew she understood the importance of moving fast. Problem was, the smoke and heat brought on exhaustion. Every gesture and step seemed to take forever. It was as if they moved in slow motion.

With the small space stuffed as tight as possible, he joined her at the open double doors. A sweep of cool air hit their faces, refreshing them. He inhaled as deeply as possible, trying to draw oxygen into his body to feed his muscles and brain. He needed all his strength and wits for the next few minutes. He could not afford to have a weak arm and a stilted mind.

He also needed Claire to trust him. "Listen to me."

"We're trapped in here."

"No, we're not. We can get out."

"How?"

"We're going over the side."

She walked to the front of the balcony and looked at the ground below. "It's a long way down."

"It's fine."

She checked the distance again. "Probably twenty feet."

From what he could tell, more like thirty.

"We'll make it." He used his most assured tone.

If she sensed his fear, they'd never make it. He knew from her reactions of the past that heights made her nervous. Add in the fire and choking smoke and she'd venture into full panic mode.

Besides, he was already worried about how he would support his weight with one good arm. There was no way he could balance both of them and get them to safety. No, she had to do her part.

The two of them. Together.

"I'm afraid of heights." She shook her

head so hard that he waited for her to fall over. "Deathly afraid."

"You're more afraid of dying. Trust me."

"I can't jump." Her mouth flattened. "Don't ask me to do this. I can't."

"Stop." He stepped in front of her.

"Please, Luke."

His palm cupped her cheek. With his thumb he rubbed a bit of soot off the tip of her nose. "We can do this. We'll lower our bodies down."

"The fire is down there."

That was his biggest fear. That he'd coax her off the side only to watch the fire steal her away from him. They could choke, miscalculate, fall. The chances for failure were too significant to contemplate. But the probability of death if they stayed in that room was a hundred percent. Even now, small curls of smoke seeped through the blanket and trickled into the room.

The sight revived his stubbornness. He would not die today. She would live to see this through.

"When we get low enough, we'll swing out and jump," he said.

"Luke, I can't…"

He pressed his forehead against hers. "There is nothing you can't do. I've never known a woman with more spirit or heart."

Her eyes turned misty as her lips moved against his.

"And I can't do this without you, Claire. If you stay, I stay. We'll face the fire together, but we will not survive."

She nibbled on her lower lip as she turned her head and glanced nervously over the side. "How do we do this?"

A thunderous roar filled the background. It sounded like ten thousand trains bearing down on them. Luke knew the sound. It meant the flames were growing and devouring. The foundation beneath would soon sway, then crumble into the killing heat.

He ran back into the room and stripped the sheets off the bed. When she saw him struggling with the elastic, she rushed over and helped. They worked in tandem, grabbing the cotton and dragging it back out with them to the balcony.

"Help me with this." He slipped his hand under the heavy bed and pulled.

"What are you doing?"

"We need to anchor the sheets on something."

Together they moved the bed, wedging it in the doorway with one end sticking out into the balcony. He took one last look around the room and decided to try one more thing. "The mattress."

"What about it?"

"We'll throw it on the ground as a precaution." He doubted it would help, but if they fell from ten feet, the padding should help.

"I'll trust you."

He hoped that wouldn't be the biggest mistake of her life. "Good."

They picked up opposite ends. Once more the slice to his shoulder made his one hand useless. But she had enough strength for both of them. She wrapped her fingers around the handles on the side of the mattress and tugged until it almost rolled on top of her. He finished the job by chucking it over the side. It bounced, but was still within aiming distance.

"Do you know how to tie a strong knot?" she asked.

He had to smile at her attempts to stay positive in the face of doom. "I thought we'd use the sheets as parachutes and fly down."

Her hands stopped working. "That's a joke, right?"

"I'm the son of an army man. Spent my youth camping and my twenties in the military. The one thing I can do without trouble is tie a knot."

"That explains a lot about you."

"It's not news to you. You know that much of my background."

"But the context is different now."

"Okay."

"But have at it." She handed him the edges. "Be all you can be."

He tried to keep her gaze on him and her back to the door. She didn't need to see the smoke pouring in and around the makeshift blockage and slowly filling the room. He knew she could hear the house creak and moan beneath them, knew she smelled the fire and felt the heat under them. From all around, flames spit out windows and blackness filled the sky.

They had to go or risk losing their only hope.

He tightened the sheets at every juncture one last time. Unless they ripped, they should hold.

"You're going first," he said.

"No. I can follow."

"If you lead, I'll know you're out." And that would leave him as the one to fight off the flames he knew were about to knock on the door.

He already heard the shocking *whoosh* of fire as it started its race up the hallway. That meant they were dealing in seconds, instead of minutes, at this point.

When she hesitated, he slid her thigh up and onto the edge of the balcony wall. "You've got to go."

Her gaze searched his face. "Promise me you'll follow. No hero stuff."

"Absolutely."

She kissed him then, long and deep. The intensity shook him. He knew she was saying a possible goodbye.

"I love you," she whispered.

Then she lowered her body over the edge. With shaking arms and panic in her eyes, she slipped hand over hand down the side.

When her side slammed against the wall, she screamed but held on.

Fear shot through him. "You okay?"

"Yes," she said in a shaky voice.

He knew she could see the fire. Feel the extreme heat against her clothes and skin. He tried to keep her attention focused on him. "You're almost there."

She had a good thirty feet to go. The poisoned air made her cough.

But she was better down there than up here with him, so he was grateful. Fire danced up the doorway and snapped at thc ceiling.

He pulled tighter to the edge of the balcony and inhaled as much air as possible. Even that stagnated in his mouth. The air outside slowly became as polluted as the stuff behind him.

"Luke!"

Her scream had him looking down again. Flames exploded around her. He thought about jumping down there but forced his legs to stay still.

"Swing out," he yelled over the roar of the fire.

"How?"

"Move your body. Get away from the

flames." He had to curl his hands around his mouth and yell down to her. The banging and hissing from the fire almost drowned him out.

She pushed, at first barely moving. But when a cloud of smoke engulfed her, she began rocking back and forth. He helped from above by pulling the sheets away from the wall. The motion caused the bed to smack harder against the doorframe, but the knots held and the creaking wood continued to provide the needed counterbalance to her weight.

"Now, Claire. Jump."

She glanced up, her eyes filled with terror, and then nodded. He could see her take a breath. And then she let go. With a yelp, she flapped her arms and fell. When her body hit the edge of the mattress and rolled off onto the grass, he stopped breathing.

He leaned out farther and tried to make out her form through the billowing smoke. "Claire?"

"Get down here!"

Nothing subtle about that. Luke didn't wait for a second command. He curled the sheets around his good arm and threw a leg over the wall. He tugged twice to make sure he still had some leverage. Holding his body up with one hand and shimmying down wasn't going to be easy. He had to depend on open spaces against the wall to jump off and land. Then he had to hope he didn't send his body flying right into the flames.

Smoke filled the bedroom. The flames raced right behind. The bed would go up in the next few seconds.

He hopped off the edge and felt the immediate tug of his weight against the muscles in his biceps and shoulder. His bones strained and his hand blistered as he hung there.

The blaze raged around him. He couldn't even see the ground. The rumble and crack of the fire filled the area as the sky turned black with smoke.

He swung his body against an open space on the wall. With one arm, he couldn't stop his momentum and smashed into the brick wall. His grip slipped, dropping him two feet lower on the sheets.

Claire's muffled shouts reached him through the noise and madness. She was begging him to keep going.

That was the push he needed. He clutched the material tighter in his fist and used his legs to guide him down. As he hit the bottom floor of the house, all he saw was fire. It traveled everywhere, destroying everything it touched.

He hung there, fifteen feet from the ground and unable to locate the mattress, and knew the climb down was over. The fire had scorched the end of the sheets from the bottom and was moving up toward him. He bunched his body, bringing his legs up tight to his stomach, then pushed out and let go.

The tumble through the air took about a second but felt like forever. Boiling heat surrounded him. Flames inched up to touch him. He passed through it all, landing with a hard thump on the far edge of the mattress. Despite the cushion, the whack of ground against bones shocked the breath right out of him.

Claire was there to bring it back.

She gripped his arm and started pulling. "Luke, wake up."

He didn't realize his eyes were closed until she said the words. "Give me a second."

"We don't have one to spare." Her tugging became more insistent.

He looked up and saw the wall of red and orange roaring in front of them. They stood in a half circle of fire. They had a slim path out to green grass and land not seared by an uncontrolled inferno.

Finding a reserve of energy fueled only by adrenaline, he pushed to his feet and ran at a crouch with Claire by his side. The house exploded behind them as they continued to chase fresh air.

Out of danger, they fell to the hard ground and coughed out the smoke filling their lungs. Fatigue dragged at his muscles, but Luke knew they weren't done. He had lost contact with Adam and Holden. They could be anywhere, including in the middle of the hell they had just escaped.

He lost the mic during all the climbing and falling. There was only one other way to check on his friends. He found the energy to lift his arm and stare at his watch. The screen was black.

"Why aren't the fire trucks here?" Claire asked. The question came out in a rasp.

"We're far enough away from other houses that it will take time for anyone to see it."

"There's enough smoke to signal another planet."

"Well, when you hear the sirens don't get too excited."

"Why?"

"We're not supposed to be here, remember?"

"Right." She tapped her fingers against his chest. "Where do you think Steve and Phil are? The goal was to catch them. They could be anywhere."

He wished they were dead, but he knew better.

"They're running."

"I doubt they'll be as good at it as I was."

"I'm hoping they drive past Holden and he rams their car." Luke felt her shift. When he finally found the strength to open his eyes, her expression swam above him. "What? What are you thinking?"

"I've got a better idea."

"For what?"

"I know where they are."

Luke wasn't sure he knew where *he* was at this point. "How is that possible?"

"They're not driving."

"Then what are they doing?"

"How about flying?"

He lifted his head off the ground. "I don't—"

"Adam said there was a helicopter pad on the grounds."

Luke's brain cells started firing again. "Sounds convenient for the perfect getaway."

"Not if we can help it."

Chapter Sixteen

Claire stared out into the distance and tried to figure out where her evil ex-husband would hide a helicopter pad. She strained to remember if the site had shown up on the photo lineup Adam had shared with them on the laptop. She could only conjure up a blank page.

"Which way?" she asked when she couldn't come up with the direction just by willing it.

Luke's gaze wandered over the landscape before settling on the far side of what once was the house. "There."

"Are you guessing?"

"More of a deduction, actually."

"Based on?"

"I know it's not behind us and wouldn't be in the front yard. That only leaves one direction."

"That's good enough for me."

With the world exploding behind them and pieces of flaming wood and paper falling to the ground around them, they kept moving. The jog to the opposite end of the house took forever. The ache in her leg slowed them down. She kept trying to shake it off, but the crack of marble against her knee had done some damage.

Dodging behind the small outbuildings scattered around the grounds and hiding from any eyes that might be watching also limited their progress. The only good news was that the fire hadn't engulfed the older part of the house. That meant their march across the wide yard brought some fresh air and welcome relief for her dry nose and parched throat. But not much. Smoke and the charred smell seeped into everything.

When they reached the edge of the house, he pushed her back against a gardening shed. "Stop."

She didn't mind the manhandling now. Walking into the middle of a new disaster didn't appeal to her. "What do you see?"

"Two idiots loading boxes onto a helicopter."

"The other guards?"

"No, the idiots you were related to."

She peeked around the corner. On the next acre over sat the aircraft in the middle of a concrete pad. There was a small steel hangar between them and the Samson brothers. Other than that, they were looking at a wide-open field with grass that looked as if it hadn't been mowed in a month—very few places to hide.

"Can Phil fly a helicopter?" Luke asked.

"You're asking the wrong person. I didn't even know he owned this house."

"Well, there's not much left of that."

They both glanced over at what used to be a stone mansion. Now it was a ball of fire slowly collapsing in on itself on one side.

"What a waste." She thought that summed up the property, as well as the past two years.

"Yeah, someone could have used it as a hospital."

"Or a college." She left that problem and focused on the human one in front of her. "What are they doing?"

"Packing."

"What's left?"

"Whatever they need to make a run for it. Looks like they stored whatever they needed back here. The money is likely already out of the reach of the U.S. government."

"Why do you think that?"

"They wouldn't take the risk of having it with them. It's been transferred and transferred again to throw off anyone trying to track it down."

"It shouldn't be that easy."

"You'd be amazed."

"So why waste time with whatever they're doing now?"

"This is the getaway part of their plan."

"Even if they can fly that thing out, they're not going to get very far in it. They can't exactly get to South America from here." Not that she knew much about helicopters. She barely knew anything about cars except you got in and started the engine. "Right?"

"They only have to get to a private airport. That's not a problem out here in rich-people country. I'm sure there are airstrips all over the place."

"Convenient."

"And with their money they can bribe people from there, hire a flight instructor or anyone who needs some cash and get out of the country."

"I wish they'd done that from the beginning and left me alone."

"They needed you to buy time and for cover. They've been hatching this for quite some time. Hell, these two likely have had their escape all mapped out ever since they decided to take their employees' money. They knew how to get everything else done without making the police suspect them."

"I wouldn't have said they were that smart."

"Think of it as underhanded."

She watched as Phil heaved a bag onto the helicopter. "So they get to leave with all that money."

"Yeah, they think so."

"What do *you* think?"

"That we're going to stop them."

"Any idea how we do that?"

"They believe their plan worked and we're dead, so we have surprise on our side."

Luke was getting ready to pounce. The anxiety thrumming off him crashed against her. The pure predator in him shone through in every line of his body. Everything in his stance said battle. He had the prey in his sights.

His need to attack sparked hers. "We have to get out there now before they spot us or take off."

"I will."

She closed her eyes to keep from screaming. "You aren't leaving me behind and we are not going to spend two seconds arguing that point."

He nodded. "Wouldn't dream of disagreeing with you."

That was way too easy. She hadn't won a similar battle with him—ever. Now he was acquiescing to her command and smiling at her as if he'd gone simple.

She didn't trust the change one bit.

"So what *are* you dreaming about?" she asked, waiting for him to return to his me-man-you-woman-stay-here ways.

"Crawling over there, getting the jump on Phil and then using him as a shield against Steve. The goal is to keep them from lifting off and grab whatever it is they think is important enough to waste time loading on the plane."

"You think Steve is in charge." For some reason that struck her as odd. She had also viewed Phil as the more suave and sophisticated of the two.

"He's the one with the gun."

"Under that theory you're in charge."

"Yeah, let's see how that works."

Luke could shoot both men for all she cared.

"And what do I do while you're doing your superhero act across the lawn?" she asked.

He nodded to the building situated between them and the escape helicopter. "Circle around by the hangar."

"You think there's another helicopter in there?"

"I only have one gun and I'm going to need it, so you need to find a weapon."

"Like what?"

"A piece of metal. A crowbar. Anything you can carry and use to stab or hit with."

"And just who am I attacking?"

Phil. She wanted to take Phil down.

"Whichever one I leave standing," Luke said.

"Makes sense. I like the plan so far."

Luke drew a diagram on her hand with his

finger. "I go in from the front and you sneak around from the back."

When he started to kneel down and winced in the process, guilt struck her. She laid a hand against his hair. "Can you do this?"

"I'm the professional, remember?"

"You've been beaten and you fall about one story to the hard ground. Even professionals are destructible."

"You jumped and you're fine."

"I was almost at the bottom of those sheets when I let go. You were at the top."

He shook his head. "I'm fine."

That was his mantra. She now understood that he said the empty words whenever he was the exact opposite of *fine*.

But they had a bigger problem. A mess she was trying to ignore rather than risk having it stop her. But she had to deal with it. Luke's life might depend on it.

She brushed her fingers over the sticky stain on his now crusty shirt. "You have blood everywhere."

"What?" He glanced at his shoulder and frowned. "I need a new bandage."

The ultimate understatement.

The reality is that he hadn't even realized that blood poured down his arm. She guessed that the mix of danger and adrenaline kept his blood pumping and the pain at bay. Either that or he had moved into a state of advanced denial. His mind had shut off to the numbness moving through him.

His brain might be fighting the extent of his injuries, but hers wasn't. She hadn't seen him move his arm in any significant way since they got into the mansion. When he held her, he only used one hand. And watching him get down that rope while one arm dangled at his side counted as the most harrowing moment in a series of endless horrors.

Swollen fingers. Limp muscles. Blood soaking through what was once white cotton wrapped around the wound. The same material now glowing and stained with dark red.

It didn't take a doctor to know Luke was in huge physical trouble. She expected he couldn't even close his fist at this point. So she made the decision for him. Her priorities were clear now. Whatever happened to her happened. She could face jail, even a false sentence, if Luke lived. The important thing was to get him to a hospital before he lost his arm…or worse.

"We should forget about this and leave." She pointed at the figures in the distance.

"No."

"Let them get away. They don't matter now."

"Absolutely not."

"I'm sure we can track down a neighbor or passing car somewhere around here."

"I said no. Several times. I mean it. We're finishing this if it kills me."

That was her fear. "We know the truth."

Her biggest concern, greatest relief, was that Luke believe in her. She could face anything or anyone with that knowledge tucked deep in her heart.

Luke refused to listen. He shook his head. "I'm going in."

She tilted his chin so that his gaze was forced to meet hers. "It doesn't matter. Only *you* matter."

The words came from deep inside her. A tiny area she had locked out of her mind two years earlier opened. Now the truth of her feelings pumped through her, overtaking everything else.

His dark frown didn't waver. "If they get into that helicopter, I might not be able to save you."

"I'm more concerned with saving you."

She could see him wrestle with the best way to fight her terror. The tension across his shoulders eased as his palm moved up her leg. "I'm going to be here. But I'm not going to be able to live with myself if we walk away now and let these two idiots escape to freedom without being punished for what they've done to you and all their employees."

Their priorities still clashed because all she cared about was making sure Luke lived. "What if we fail?"

"We won't."

Luke was sure of that part. They had come too far to turn around and sneak off now. He didn't even know where they would go. No one was around for miles, and he didn't have the strength for a hike. He had just enough energy to take out a Samson or two. He'd worry about the rest later, because no more bags or boxes sat on the ground near the helicopter. Liftoff was imminent. Luke could feel it.

"Let's go," he said.

They took off in opposite directions. He went first, not giving her another chance to argue. If Phil and Steve were going to spot one of them, Luke wanted to make sure it was him. He didn't want to give away his position, but he would draw their gazes if necessary to protect her.

As Claire shimmied along the ground with her head down and using only her elbows and knees to propel her across the grass, Luke started jogging. He bent down as far as possible. There was no way his one side would support him long enough to get him close to the helicopter, and for his plan to work, he had to get damn close.

He stopped and dropped down, keeping as still as possible when the brothers faced the house. Their laughter filled the smoky air. Clearly they thought letting people burn to death was hilarious.

It only made Luke hate them more.

Luke used that fury to push himself on.

His body ran only on the drive to see these men caught and Claire's name cleared.

When the laughter stopped, Luke lifted his head again. He saw a flash of white off to his right as Claire stood up and slipped behind the hangar. That meant it was his turn to act.

He waited until the brothers turned and looked over the booty in the helicopter. There wouldn't be another chance. Luke inhaled and took off. He ran as fast as he could, using up every energy reserve inside him to get to the two men.

As he shot across the clear field toward Phil, Steve pivoted. Shock registered on the older man's face and he gave a shout of warning. Phil proved slower. He raised his hands to his head as if ducking from a flying object but didn't get out of Luke's path.

Knocking the man down would satisfy the desire to hurt him, but Luke doubted he could get back up once he was down. That would leave him vulnerable to attack by two men who would think nothing of beating him to death with their hands. Instead, he used all his concentration to slam his body to a halt.

He slowed his movements in time to raise his gun and shove it into the back of Phil's head. Phil screamed in rage.

When Luke turned his gaze to Steve, Luke saw the gun. So while Luke pointed his gun at Phil, Steve pointed his at Luke. It was a circle of violence that guaranteed at least two of them would end up dead. Luke knew which two he would pick.

"Drop it or I'll kill your brother." The blood pounded hard enough through Luke's body to threaten to knock him down.

Steve's mouth twisted in a snarl. "You don't have it in you."

"You don't know me."

Phil cowered under the gun. "Where's Claire?"

The question proved she'd made it to the hangar without being seen. These two had lied their way through their entire plan, but Luke sensed this was not a trick. So he adopted their skills.

"She's in a room on the second floor of your house. And you're going to pay for her death." He laid the desperate act on thick, playing the role of a heartbroken and deranged boyfriend. It wasn't hard to conjure up the feelings, because he had been toying with them all day.

"He's lying," Phil said as he tried to move away from the gun.

Luke pulled him back, shoving the gun harder against Phil's skull. "You aren't in a position to question."

"But I am." Calm washed over Steve. He acted like a man in control rather than a man who got caught.

"It's over, Steve. You lost."

"No. Phil did."

A shot rang out. For a second Luke wondered if he had fired by accident. Then he saw Phil lying at his feet. Drops of blood sprayed in a pattern across Luke's shirt. He looked at his stomach and at Phil's still body and realized the blood wasn't his.

Steve's skills were as impressive as Luke feared. Steve had put a bullet right through the center of his brother's black heart.

"You shot him." The idea was so outrageous that Luke's mind refused to grasp it.

"He served his purpose."

The men now held guns on each other.

"Which was?"

"To set up Claire and grab the money." Steve shifted so that the helicopter sat directly behind him, as if he wanted something hard supporting his back.

"You used him."

"He's always been the brother for show. I'm the brother for action."

"You're the murderer."

Steve laughed without amusement. "This, too, will fall on Claire."

"She's dead."

"That's just part of the cover-up. Once again Claire has complied with my wishes and performed in a way that only makes the story better."

"What are you talking about?"

The dead woman in question slipped behind the helicopter. Luke saw a flash of her hair and the edge of her shirt before she disappeared behind her metal cover again. Knowing she was there made his fingers tighten on the gun. She had walked right into the middle of a lethal situation, but having her on his team might be their only chance.

"In my story she dies while trying to get away and everything goes wrong."

"It will never work."

"Sure it will. The public already sees her as a killer. Adding Phil's death now is perfect. It will make it look as if she kept him alive and only now killed him." Steve's arm stiffened.

"You shoot, I shoot."

"You are a minute away from dropping on top of Phil. Just look at you. How much blood have you lost by now? A pint? More? That brain of yours will shut down soon."

As Steve said the words, Luke's muscles grew weak. "Not before I kill you."

"If you kill me, how do you clear your precious Claire's name?"

"That doesn't matter now."

"Steve!" Claire shouted his name in a quick burst and without giving away her exact position.

Surprise had Steve turning around, which was all Luke needed. He aimed and fired straight into Steve's back. The shot propelled Steve's body forward and his gun dropped from his fingers to the grass.

"No..." Steve slumped over the opening

area in the center of the helicopter before falling on his back to the ground.

Luke watched the man's eyes flutter and his chest heave for breaths. A bloodstain spread over his stomach as his face went pale.

Luke took it all in, tried to care. But he couldn't feel anything, didn't even know how he kept standing. He heard bells and whistles and thought he had to be hallucinating. His mind had finally checked out as his body went numb.

Claire appeared at his side. "Luke?"

She was okay. He repeated that fact over and over.

"I'm right here." Her hands traveled over his chest and across his face.

He saw rather than felt her touch. "Claire?"

"The police are coming. I can hear the sirens."

"Were you hurt?"

"No." She wrapped an arm around his waist. "Hold on."

"Can't."

And then his world went black.

Chapter Seventeen

The next few minutes passed in a whirl. The wind kicked up as a fleet of police cars raced across the lawn. They stopped, kicking up dust around Claire and stopping only inches from where she lay covering Luke's still body on the ground.

"Help me!"

Doors opened. Holden and Adam stepped out. When Holden tried to run to her, two officers had to hold him back.

"Get down." The policeman's order boomed across her senses.

His words confused her. The danger from Steve and Phil had passed. Why weren't they coming to Luke? "He needs an ambulance."

"Step away from him."

The command didn't make any sense. She

was saving him, keeping him and protecting him from additional pain. Trying to stop the bleeding from his arm.

She continued to kneel on the ground. "What are you saying?"

"Stand up."

"I don't understand."

"Claire, move away from Luke so we can get to him." Holden's mouth pulled tight as he yelled the command.

She could see the tension in the police officers surrounding her with guns raised. Adam practically bounced as he shifted and moved around, his gaze never leaving Luke.

They were here to arrest her.

The thought had her gasping. "Luke needs help!"

An officer approached her. "Put your hands up."

She obeyed even though it killed her to let go of Luke. "Please. He needs a doctor."

"I know, ma'am." The officer motioned for her to stand up. "I'm going to get him in an ambulance right now."

That promise was all she needed. She struggled to her feet with her hands in the air.

As soon as she stood, the officer grabbed her arms and wrenched them behind her.

"Careful," Holden said.

"I know how to do my job, sir." Cuffs snapped on her wrists as two ambulances raced into the yard.

An officer checked Steve's pulse. "He's alive."

No, that was wrong. She didn't care about him. No one should care about him.

"Luke goes first," she insisted.

Holden and Adam surrounded their friend until the ambulance crew shooed them away. The world erupted in chaos. Fire engines screamed around the back of the house. Men filed out with hoses and ladders and assessed the burning building. Police and emergency workers filled every inch of the grassy area she'd initially seen as huge and open. A crew worked on Steve and another on Luke.

The relief of having made it out alive made the ground spin in front of her. She almost fell, but the officer caught her against his chest and guided her to the side of his car.

"Are you hurt?" the officer asked.

"Just save Luke." She whispered the plea

as she watched the workers load Luke onto the stretcher.

Holden's face appeared in front of her. "Are you okay?"

"Luke?"

"They're working on him." Holden leaned in closer. "Do you need a medic?"

"No." She wanted all their attention on Luke.

The area around Holden's mouth whitened. "I'm sorry."

"For what?"

"I brought the police. We saw the fire and took out two of Phil's men as they ran out the front. But we couldn't get to you. We didn't know where you were in there."

She couldn't grasp what he was trying to say. She got that he'd called the ambulance. She was grateful for his quick thinking. Luke's safety was all that mattered to her.

Holden put his hands on her shoulders and gave her a little squeeze. "They're going to arrest you. I had to get them here fast and to do that I turned on you."

Now it made sense. He thought she had planned to run and he was willing to look the other way to let her go. "I'm not leaving Luke."

Holden smiled then. "Good."

LUKE FORCED his eyes open to wake up from the floating sensation cocooning his body. He saw Adam and medics. Not the one person he wanted.

"Where's Claire?" When no one paid attention to him, he said it again in a louder voice.

"Luke." Adam rushed to his side. "Are you okay?"

"Claire."

Adam's frown didn't ease. "We have to get you to a hospital."

Why wasn't he answering? "Fine. Tell me about Claire."

"Your sleeve is soaked with blood and your skin is whiter than milk. Hell, you passed out."

Luke swallowed, then pushed more strength into his voice. "I want Claire."

Adam hesitated before motioning to a police officer that Luke could see on the periphery of his vision. The ambulance crew poked and adjusted equipment. Someone took his pulse. Another guy administered a shot.

Luke didn't feel any of it. He wanted Claire by his side. Now.

A medic stepped back and Claire filled the space. Her tears fell on his face. "I'm right here."

He tried to lift his fingers to touch her lips, but his arms refused to move. "Are you okay?"

"I'm fine," she said, repeating his words.

A policeman appeared over her shoulder. "Ma'am, you need to come with us."

Irrational panic filled Luke's senses. He knew if she stepped away, he might not see her again. He could not lose her now.

"She stays with me."

"Do you have to do this now?" Holden's voice rose above the flurry of sounds and buzzing of people around him. "He needs her."

"There's a warrant out for her arrest. She's a flight risk," the officer explained.

Luke blinked, trying to fight off the lethargy stealing over him. "For what?"

"The murder of Phillip Samson," the officer said in a firm voice.

"That's Phil Samson." Holden pointed at the man's body, which hadn't moved or been moved since Luke dropped him there. "She couldn't have killed him before because he was only killed just now."

"His brother did it," Claire said in a rush.

The officer shook his head. "I have to do what I'm told."

The medic gave Luke another shot. Luke tried to tell him not to, but his tongue went numb, so he stuck with the words he needed to say. "Listen to me."

Claire leaned down and pressed her cheek against his for a second. Then she gave him a soft, loving kiss. "Luke, it's okay."

"You didn't do it."

"I know."

"You aren't going to jail."

With a nod to the medic, Holden slipped his hand under Claire's elbow and pulled her back. "We'll straighten all this out later."

Now, it had to be now. Luke tried to raise his head. The move forced bile up the back of his throat until it threatened to choke him.

The medic eased Luke back down with a

hand on his chest. "Sir, I need you to stay down."

Luke let his head fall back. "Not until I know she's coming with me."

The officer started to tug her out of the way. "She has to ride in the car."

"Holden, stop this."

Holden's mouth pinched. "Man, I can't do that. I tried."

"I can't..." Whatever the medic shot into Luke's veins now held his mind captive. Colors swirled in front of his eyes. "Claire."

"I'm here, Luke," Claire whispered.

"Come with me."

"I'll be there as soon as I can." Her voice grew more distant.

"Luke, man, you need to let the ambulance take you," Adam said.

Luke let his eyes close, but he could hear his friends arguing over him.

"Is he going to be okay?" Claire asked, her voice higher than usual and her concern evident.

"There's been a serious loss of blood." Luke didn't recognize the speaker. He assumed it was the medic, but he couldn't open his eyes to check.

"I can go with her to the police station and work this out." Luke whispered the suggestion as his body fought off the start of a gentle sleep.

"You're going into surgery. We'll stay with Claire," Holden said as he squeezed his friend's good shoulder.

"Don't let anything happen to her." Luke's breath turned shallow. "Phil tried to kill her."

"He's dead now," Claire said.

"I can't stay awake." The words came out so staggered that the sentence took forever for Luke to say.

"Don't fight it, sir." The medic slipped a mask over Luke's face.

"Where's Claire?" he mumbled.

"You'll see her soon." Holden cleared his throat. "Promise."

Luke wanted to believe, but his mind went blank.

Chapter Eighteen

Claire sat on the hard bench and dropped her head into her hands. Her fingers snagged on a piece of scorched paper between the strands. She brushed it out but did wonder what else could be caught up in there. It was a miracle she had any hair left after the fire and everything else that had happened.

Not that her looks mattered all that much where she was. After the fires and gun battles, pain and terror, she'd ended up in the one place she most feared and was desperate to avoid. A jail cell.

She had been there all night. They said she'd move to more permanent quarters today, but it hadn't happened.

Now she feared she'd be there forever, lost in the system and discarded.

Metal clanked against metal as doors opened and closed. Officers walked the area, ignoring the women confined inside. Every now and then the loudspeaker would squawk. The announcer would say a name or give an order.

Claire could barely hear the announcements over her fellow inmates' shouting and swearing. There were those who blamed the system and the men in their lives for their temporary homes behind bars. A few threw insults from their individual holding cells. She had been called a whole host of names that she sure hoped didn't fit.

She felt small and alone. Pain knocked against the back of her head, and her lungs still ached from the intake of so much smoke. An officer promised her medical attention, but she knew that would be a long wait. She was not a priority.

The press, public and prosecutor still saw her as a criminal. The arrest warrant had been issued while she ran around the Virginia countryside trying to track down Phil and prove he was alive. He wasn't dead when she got charged. He was very dead now.

She tried to care but couldn't. He had destroyed so much, stolen from everyone and wrecked something very precious about her belief in her own instincts. Innocent people in his company would wake up in a few days and find out that not only was their employer out of business, but their money was gone. Some would blame her, but they would learn the truth eventually.

Adam said it could be months or longer before law enforcement and a host of computer specialists would track down the funds. Even then, most of it could be gone. No one knew how much Phil and Steve had spent, and Steve wasn't talking.

That wasn't true. He kept babbling, insisting that she was in on it with Phil. That he was the aggrieved and innocent party. The man could lie without blinking. He'd tried to kill her and acted as if that little piece of information didn't matter.

But Steve wasn't the man she was thinking about right then. If she could manage it, she planned to never think of him again.

She wanted Luke.

Strapped to a gurney, he had disappeared

into an ambulance as the police dragged her away. She could still hear his desperate calls for her as the ambulance door shut. Just thinking about him, about them, about all they had survived and the slogging road to recovery still ahead, brought tears to her eyes. She couldn't let them fall. If her new bunkmates saw her as scared or weak, they'd attack. And she had been battered and bruised enough to last a lifetime.

"You asleep in there?" Luke's voice carried a touch of amusement.

But that couldn't be. He was in the hospital under anesthesia and observation. Adam told her about the surgery and the long recovery ahead. All while she was awaiting transfer to the cell that would become her home until her trial.

She raised her head, prepared to see nothing but bars lined up before her. But the fantasy remained. What greeted her made everything else slip away. Luke. Standing there in jeans and a clean shirt. Leaning against the open cell door with a sexy, stupid grin on his face.

She blinked a few times to make sure he

didn't vanish like the vision she'd had of him so many times during the long night. "What are you doing here?"

"It's visiting hours."

She looked down but she didn't have a watch. "Isn't it after midnight?"

"Yeah." He pushed away from the door and came closer.

She'd forgotten how big he was. His broad chest blocked the view of everything behind him. But that handsome face had never left her memory.

"You're supposed to be in the hospital."

"Holden broke me out."

"Adam said—"

"I'm fine. And this time I mean it."

"Are you allowed to be here?" she asked because she didn't know what else to say.

He had cleaned up and showered. She had fire refuse poking out of her hair and a mix of grass stains and soot caking her pants. Her fingernails were filthy. Basically, she was the least attractive person in the jail. Ever.

He walked into the cell and didn't stop until the tips of his shoes tapped against her sneakers. "I have to say this isn't exactly the response I expected when I paid your bail."

She laughed even though the joke wasn't all that funny. "It's set at a million dollars."

"It was. Not now."

"You're serious."

"I know some people."

"Sure you do."

"You doubt me?" He dropped down next to her, ignoring the catcalls from the cells around them.

"What are we talking about here?"

"You getting out of here."

The words sounded so good to her ears. "Is that ever going to happen?"

"It can happen as soon as you stand up."

He wasn't kidding. She felt that certainty through every vein. "What's going on? I'm supposed to switch to the prison. You're supposed to be resting with nurses buzzing all around you."

"Nurses are overrated. I prefer strong beautiful women who know how to create a distraction in a crisis."

Her mind still couldn't process the barrage of information hitting it. "I don't get it."

"There's a judge who owes me a favor." Luke rubbed his good shoulder against her dirty one. "Found his niece last year, kept her out of trouble and her name out of the news."

"Really?"

"He returned the favor with a reduction in bail."

She didn't understand much about the legal system, but she knew nothing worked that easily. Not at midnight on a Tuesday. "The prosecutor agreed to that?"

"He's not dumb."

"I'm sorry to hear that, since he'll be on the other side of my case."

"When I gave my statement, when Holden and Adam chimed in, it was hard for the prosecutor to hold on to the theory that you're the bad guy in this scenario."

Hope jumped to life inside her. "He believes I'm innocent?"

"He trusts me, and for now, that's good enough."

"Does that mean he dropped thc charges?" She was afraid to hope for such a fantastic ending to such a tragic series of events.

"No. Apparently I'm not that convincing."

Luke laid his hand over her knee. “But he will. He just needs a little time to check into everything. He’s satisfied that you’re done running.”

“I am.”

“Good.”

With those simple words, something important passed between them. Something strong and binding that she grabbed on to and held tight to her heart.

The brush of his thumb on her leg lulled her into a certain peace. “That feels good.”

He smiled. “It will take some more time to ferret things out. Steve is still a powerful man. The prosecutor will want everything set before he leaves you alone and turns on Steve.”

“But he will?”

“I promise.”

She wove her fingers through his and laid her head on his shoulder. The familiar snuggle gave her the security she needed to believe the court might someday untangle the mess the Samson brothers had made. And the touch of Luke’s skin against hers took the final edge off her frazzled nerves.

His sling rested against his stomach. She skimmed her fingers over it, careful not to press too hard. She had inflicted enough damage and didn't want to be responsible for one drop more.

"What did the doctor say?" she asked.

"He thinks I got shot in the shoulder."

She squeezed Luke's hand. "I meant the prognosis."

"It's fine."

She heard the edge to his voice and stared up at him, really looked into those intelligent green eyes. His smile looked forced.

She knew he had fallen back on old habits. "Tell me the truth."

"I guess I can't convince you this isn't important."

"The fact you're trying so hard not to answer is my first clue that it is."

He blew out a long breath. "Well, it would appear that running around with a shoulder injury and hanging off the side of a building are not good things. Who knew?"

"You did." She played with his hair where it curled at his ear.

"It was worth the risk."

"I'm not convinced that's true."

He shifted until she could see every inch

of his handsome face. "So that we're clear, I would do it all again if it meant that you lived. That was my only goal."

A chorus of *ahhh*s sounded from behind them, but Claire tuned them out.

"Funny, but I had a similar goal."

"Then we agree."

She saw the tactic and blocked it. "You're stalling. Tell me what this injury means for your future."

"Even in jail I can't throw you off the scent."

"No."

"It's nothing serious." He toyed with her fingers. "Some physical therapy."

There was more. With them there was always more. "And?"

"There's a possibility of some loss of use. Slight."

"Oh, Luke." An unexpected sadness surged through her. He hadn't taken care of himself, hadn't thought his injury was a big deal, because he'd been too busy taking care of her.

"No, it's okay."

But it wasn't. "I'm so sorry."

She felt the apology with every cell of her

body. If she could give him back a whole shoulder, she would.

He frowned at her. “Don’t do that.”

His change of tone to something harsh and unbending surprised her. “What?”

“Take the blame.” He lifted their joined hands to his mouth and kissed her fingers. “I was where I wanted to be.”

“You didn’t ask to be shot.”

“You didn’t ask to be framed, so we’re even.”

He just kept giving and she didn’t know how to accept it. “How can you say that?”

“Because the injury doesn’t matter.”

That wasn’t true. His job defined and motivated him. She remembered the day he’d started this position. Their dating had moved from casual to something much more, and then his work life fell into place. At the time she thought it was a desk job in antiques and couldn’t understand why shuffling papers filled him with such energy. Now that she knew his real job, she knew the real man needed the thrill and the rush.

“The job, my shoulder, none of that is really about my future.”

"What do you mean?"

He rolled his eyes. "You really don't know?"

"Apparently not."

"*You* are my future." He said it emphatically, as if daring her to test him.

She could feel the force of his will. See the determination in his eyes and hear it in his rough voice. This promise meant more than the proposal and the beautiful diamond he'd once slipped on her finger.

Now she needed him to understand. "When I apologized, it was for everything."

"I know."

"For leaving."

He shook his head. "I pushed you away. I grew up with a certain set of rules and understandings. My dad did his work and I didn't question it. I thought that's the way it should be."

"I could have kept trying."

"I wanted to blame you for all of it, but we both messed up. We both need to own that and learn from it."

"Then I apologize for coming back and dragging you into this huge mess of a life of mine."

"No, you're wrong on that one. Returning to me is the best thing you ever did."

She gnawed on her bottom lip, trying to find the right words. When they didn't come, she went with what lived in her heart. "I can't promise that the nerves won't come again, that I won't get angry and demand you give me more. The need for trust and stability is ingrained in me. For so long I was denied both. I just don't want to live like that again."

There. She'd said it. She knew what she needed to stay grounded. Now *he* knew.

He gave her a blank stare. Seconds ticked by as she waited for him to say something. Anything.

"Will you leave me when I act like a jerk?" he asked.

The breath she was holding burst out of her lungs. "No. Never."

"That's all that matters."

Wave after wave of happiness crashed over her. "So you're willing to wait until I break out of here to start something special?"

"We already have something special."

When his lips met hers and the women in the cells cheered, she lost the last tethers to her control. Playing it cool didn't suit her. She wanted him to feel how much she loved him.

She wrapped her arms around his neck and kissed him back. Kissed him with all the feeling and joy she had bottled up for the two years they'd been apart. Kissed him for all they would have and for the hurts of the past. Kissed him in a promise of forever.

When she eased back, letting their mouths gently pull apart as their breaths still mixed, she whispered her vow. "I love you.

He brushed his thumb over her lips. "I've always loved you. I'll love you forever. When you act smart or stupid, when you yell or we make love, I'm going to keep on loving you."

She couldn't stop the huge smile that formed on her face. "I think we found something else we agree on."

He pressed a second, less heated kiss against her mouth before coming back up for air again. "And now I'm going to take you home and show you."

"I can leave?" She hated to hope just in case the police officer in charge said no. But

Luke's smile told her he had worked out every angle. "What did you do?"

"Didn't I tell you?" He brushed her hair out of her face. "In addition to the bail decrease, the prosecutor released you into my custody."

She loved how that sounded. "So I'm your responsibility now."

"That's what they told me."

"You think you can handle that?"

Luke winked at her. "With you I can do anything."

"Then take me home."

* * * * *

Harlequin offers a romance
for every mood!
See below for a sneak peek from our
paranormal romance line,
Silhouette® Nocturne™.
Enjoy a preview of REUNION
by USA TODAY
bestselling author Lindsay McKenna.

Aella closed her eyes and sensed a distinct shift, like movement from the world around her to the unseen world.

She opened her eyes. And had a slight shock at the man standing ten feet away. He wasn't just any man. Her heart leaped and pounded. He reminded her of a fierce warrior from an ancient civilization. Incan? She wasn't sure but she felt his deep power and masculinity.

I'm Aella. Are you the guardian of this sacred site? she asked, hoping her telepathy was strong.

Fox's entire body soared with joy. Fox struggled to put his personal pleasure aside.

Greetings, Aella. I'm the assistant guardian to this sacred area. You may call me Fox. How can I be of service to you, Aella? he asked.

I'm searching for a green sphere. A legend says that the Emperor Pachacuti had seven emerald spheres created for the Emerald Key necklace. He had seven of his priestesses and priests travel the world to hide these spheres from evil forces. It is said that when all seven spheres are found, restrung and worn, that Light will return to the Earth. The fourth sphere is here, at your sacred site. Are you aware of it? Aella held her breath. She loved looking at him, especially his sensual mouth. The desire to kiss him came out of nowhere.

Fox was stunned by the request. *I know of the Emerald Key necklace because I served the emperor at the time it was created. However, I did not realize that one of the spheres is here.*

Aella felt sad. Why? Every time she looked at Fox, her heart felt as if it would tear out of her chest. *May I stay in touch with you as I work with this site?* she asked.

Of course. Fox wanted nothing more than

to be here with her. To absorb her ephemeral beauty and hear her speak once more.

Aella's spirit lifted. What *was* this strange connection between them? Her curiosity was strong, but she had more pressing matters. In the next few days, Aella knew her life would change forever. How, she had no idea....

Look for REUNION
by USA TODAY *bestselling author*
Lindsay McKenna,
available April 2010, only from
Silhouette® Nocturne™.

Harlequin® Historical
Historical Romantic Adventure!

...there's more to the story!

Superromance.
A *big* satisfying read about unforgettable characters. Each month we offer *six* very different stories that range from family drama to adventure and mystery, from highly emotional stories to romantic comedies—and much more! Stories about people you'll believe in and care about. Stories too compelling to put down....

Our authors are among today's *best* romance writers. You'll find familiar names and talented newcomers. Many of them are award winners—and you'll see why!

If you want the biggest and best in romance fiction, you'll get it from Superromance!

Exciting, Emotional, Unexpected...

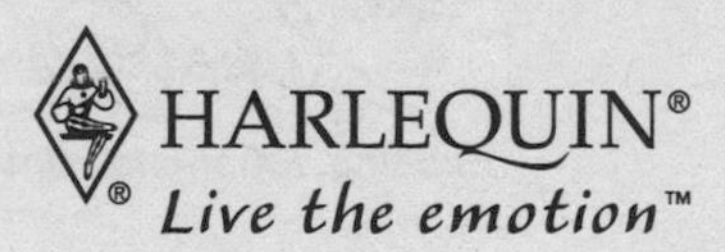

www.eHarlequin.com

HSDIR06